THE BOWL
OF
NIGHT

Also by Rosemary Edghill

SPEAK DAGGERS TO HER
BOOK OF MOONS

THE BOWL OF NIGHT

NIGHT

A BAST MYSTERY

Rosemary
Edghill

A Tom Doherty Associates Book
New York

THE BOWL OF NIGHT

This book is printed on acid-free paper.

A Forge Book
Published by Tom Doherty Associates, Inc.
175 Fifth Avenue
New York, NY 10010

Forge® is a registered trademark of Tom Doherty Associates, Inc.

Library of Congress Cataloging-in-Publication Data

Edghill, Rosemary.
    The bowl of night: a Bast mystery / by Rosemary Edghill.
      p.   cm.
    "A Tom Doherty Associates Book."
    ISBN 0-312-85606-7
    1. Women detectives—New York (State)—New York—Fiction.
    2. Occultism—New York (State)—New York—Fiction. I. Title.
PS3555.D475B69   1996
813'.54—dc20   96-8299
                                CIP

First Edition: October 1996

Printed in the United States of America

0 9 8 7 6 5 4 3 2 1

Acknowledgments

No book is written in a vacuum, especially a mystery, since inside a vacuum, it's too dark to type. Once again, I'd like to thank those who helped:

H. Dixon Smith III, Lieutenant, Dutchess County Sheriff's Department, Poughkeepsie, NY, for helping me with what must have seemed to him to be endless procedural questions. Everything pertaining to sheriffs that has an air of authenticity in this manuscript is due to his patient help. The errors, of course, remain entirely mine.

R. Stevens (for arming my deputies and providing 10-codes at short notice)

Adam Pacio (for griffin-back aerial support)

Esther Friesner (nobody expects the Spanish Disquisition)

Greer Gilman (for the gates of hell)

Myra Morales and Jennara Wenk (for prufrutting above and beyond the call of duty)

And, as always, to Greg Cox, my editor, who is never less than a pleasure to work with.

Awake! for Morning in the Bowl of Night
Has flung the Stone that puts the Stars to Flight

—*The Rubáiyát* (FitzGerald 1859 translation)

THE BOWL
OF
NIGHT

I

I hate Halloween. This might seem odd, but only consider how many people profess to hate Christmas — that frenzied end-of-year potlatch that has dragged Hanukkah down with it in a fine Judeo-Christian unanimity. December 25's certainly not a religious holiday anymore, and if not for the fact that retailers do 50 percent of their annual business during the month of December, the observance might actually die out. One of my co-workers defines Christmas as "The time of year when you buy people you don't like things they don't want with money you don't have" — which seems, on the face of it, to be a pretty good description of the entire winter gift-giving season, Kwanzaa included.

That much being said, I should also add that while it is actually possible for me to ignore the debasement of Hanukkah/Christmas/Kwanzaa/Yule (having no one to buy presents for), I have no such luck with Halloween. All Hallows' Eve is, after all, the climax of what passes for the liturgical year in our Community, and so I loathe the Real World "celebration" of it from the first sighting of Halloween candy at the grocery store to the last newspaper story about holiday vandalism; from the cute stories about Wiccans in your local newspaper to the green-faced

Margaret Hamilton clones on every door, window, and trick-or-treat bag.

Those of you who hate Christmas will understand; I cling to the reactionary position that religious holidays—like Halloween—are not shopping opportunities. But then, my name is Bast, and I'm a Witch.

I don't want your ruby slippers, and you and your little dog can live in perfect harmony for all of me; what Hollywood means and what I mean by the "W" word are miles apart. What Hollywood means—after Bette Midler's last flop—is that bucktoothed broads on broomsticks are box-office poison. What I mean is that I'm a practitioner of a NeoPagan Earth-centered religion—Wicca—the majority of whose practitioners define themselves as Witches and then spend tedious hours on the political reeducation of everyone within earshot.

Not me. I'm a Witch, but I won't go on about my religion if you don't go on about yours. And like you, there are times when I don't think about my religion at all and times when I actually feel like an oppressed minority.

Times like Halloween. Or as we call it, Samhain.

In most Wiccan traditions, Samhain (pronounced "Sowwan," for those of you who didn't grow up speaking Gaelic) is the Feast of the Dead; the festival at which we followers of Wiccan and NeoPagan traditions remember our beloved dead, whether tied to us by kinship or simply by affinity. It is also the time, both in Christian traditions and ours, when the world of the dead and the world of the living draw together, and when past and future merge, just for an instant.

Or, in modern terms, it's a time for wholesale vandalism and the mass purchase of cheap candy.

My personal rebellion against the secular commercialization of Samhain has taken the form, for the past thirteen years, of an escape to HallowFest.

HallowFest is a Pagan gathering held on Columbus

Day (observed) weekend at the Paradise Lake Campground in Gotham County, New York. A Pagan festival has certain things in common with a Christian religious retreat, except that HallowFest isn't restricted to one denomination, or even to one religion. People come from all over the eastern seaboard and from as far west as Ohio and Indiana; it's a Samhain celebration for most of us, but it isn't held Halloween weekend, because covens hold their private celebrations then.

This was the first year I wouldn't have a coven to go to—or with. I was hoping HallowFest would help me forget about all that. And as it turned out, it did; a salutary lesson in being very careful about what you wish for.

But that was later. This was Friday, and all I was thinking about when I got up that morning was getting to Paradise Lake, which is about two hours' drive north of NYC on a good day.

Holding the thought of our planned two P.M. departure firmly in mind, I'd gotten myself and my duffel bag down to The Serpent's Truth promptly at eleven o'clock. Julian was just opening up. The van, which someone had been supposed to fetch earlier and leave parked out front, was nowhere to be seen.

The Snake (or, technically, Tree of Wisdom, the Snake's mail-order branch) has a table every year at HallowFest, selling those things—from Dragon's Blood resin to crystals to purpose-built athamés—that attending Pagans can't find in their own backyards. Most years I drive the van, driver's licenses being in short supply among New Yorkers. Most years, I take one of the clerks from the store. This year I was taking Julian.

Yes indeed, Julian: ceremonial magician, my clandestine lust-object, and neurasthenic manager of New York's oldest and tackiest occult bookstore, The Serpent's Truth—known to its intimates as The Snake. Julian the Un-Pagan was coming to HallowFest—for some reason having nothing to do with my company, sanity prompted me to suppose.

"Hi, Julian," I said brightly. He ignored this, but Julian tends to do this with conversation not to his taste. I stashed my duffel behind the counter and looked around. The stock for HallowFest, which ought by rights to have been already packed, seemed still to be on the shelves.

"So, are we ready to go?" I chirped, just to be difficult. We weren't ready to go. We'd never been ready to go on schedule in living memory. The festival didn't really open until tomorrow, but Summerisle Coven was running the festival this year and I knew Maidjene, its High Priestess, would let us come in and set up early.

"Here are the keys," Julian said, handing me the keys, parking voucher, and registration for the van.

Julian is an entirely satisfactory manager for the Snake, looking, as he does, as if he might have stepped full-blown from a nineteenth-century Russian icon, from his lank black hair and steel-rimmed bifocals to his rusty hammertail coat. He wears a Roman collar, too, which he may be entitled to, for all I know. But he doesn't drive.

I headed for the subway. Maybe he and Brianna would pack while I was gone.

I doubted it, of course, but it was possible.

The Snake's van is an ancient Ford, once black and now mostly primer gray, in a dramatic state of disrepair and with most of the lower body panels rusted through. Driving it is an adventure. Between the subways, the garage, and New York traffic—factoring in a stop for gas because anytime I get my hands on the van the tank is nearly empty—I got back to the Snake around one-thirty.

There was no legal parking left on the street. I double-parked in front of the shop and went in. Julian was just giving instructions to Brianna, the clerk of the moment, on how to handle the store while Julian—its manager—was gone.

Brianna is short, round, dreamy-eyed, and vague to a fault. She also has black hair long enough to sit on, something that I was pretty sure was not a factor in any decision of Julian's or Tris's (the Snake's actual owner) to keep her, considering Tris's sexual preferences and the fact that Julian is not known to have any, alas. Her continued employment is far likelier to be because Brianna shows up (eventually), is willing to work for something less than minimum wage, and doesn't steal.

"This key locks the top lock," Julian was saying patiently.

"Um-m," said Brianna.

Tris (it's short for Trismegistus, and probably not the name he was born with) usually hangs around when Julian isn't here, so there wasn't much chance for Brianna to get into serious trouble, but Julian is nothing if not thorough.

"The van is double-parked out front," I said at a suitable break in the conversation.

Brianna's gaze slowly wandered toward me. Her eyes are an unlikely shade of turquoise, which is natural so far as I know. There was a pause while she adjusted to the fact of my presence.

"I guess we better start packing the stuff for the festival?" she said at last.

In other words, business as usual.

I could tell myself I was putting up with this monstrous lack of organization for the pleasure of Julian's company, but the fact is that I do it every year whether he's going or not. It would be a real stretch to call this community service—and I'm not much on altruism anyway—so the only possible explanation must be masochism. As masochistic experiences go, this was a pretty good one; it was about four o'clock when Brianna,

Julian, and I finally started loading cartons of books, Tarot cards, and Pagan jewelry into the van. The work went fast; Julian is stronger than he looks. But it was eight by the time he and I were well and truly rolling.

It was dark by the time we'd crossed the Willis Avenue Bridge (one of my favorite bridges, owing to the fact that the City of New York, in its infinite wisdom, has chosen to paint it a pale violet) and progressed, toll free (another reason I like the Willis), to the Governor Thomas E. Dewey Thruway (or *Twy*, according to the signs). Although this meant there wasn't much to see in the way of scenery unless you liked strip-malls and headlights, I still felt that same deviant thrill that leaving the metroplex for the land where the green things grow always gives me.

Once you become used to Manhattan's asphalt ecosphere, there is something perversely unnatural about suburbia, a land characterized by shopping malls and meaningless expanses of lawn. By comparison, there's something reasonable about the true countryside—which is defined as anything above commuting range.

We cut over from the thruway to the Sawmill River Parkway, stopped once for dinner at a Chinese place in Tarrytown (New Yorkers preferring their native cuisine whenever possible), once for gas when the tank got to half full, and once for groceries, because HallowFest is a demi-camping event: without tenting but with the necessity of preparing most of your own meals. In practice, this means I exist for three days on trail mix, tinned smoked oysters, and warm Diet Pepsi. Julian bought vegetables.

After that, we got lost—which was also a part of my yearly HallowFest experience, although it is something I try to avoid each time. All I know is that we reached New Paltz just fine and after that all is darkness.

Paradise Lake Campground does not, to my knowledge, waste money on advertising. There is only one small sign visible from County 6, and that sign directs you not to the campground, but up a long, twisting, one-and-a-half-lane road that goes on long enough for you to be sure you've missed your way. It is especially easy to think that at 12:30 in the morning after having been certain you were going the right way twice before.

Should you demonstrate the proper perseverance, the one-and-a-half-lane road offers you the opportunity to turn onto a one-lane dirt road with a hand-painted sign on it which merely says "Office." We passed "Office" a few minutes later, driving slowly because of the ruts in the road and the state of the van's suspension.

The Paradise Lake Campground consists of approximately one hundred acres, most of which are scrub, second-growth timber, and marsh. There is, as advertised, a lake, in which you can even swim if you are less squeamish about our woodland friends—leeches, water moccasins, and large pike—than I am. There are also outdoor accommodations for oh, say, 250 tent-and-RV campers on the meadow surrounding the lake, but the real reason that HallowFest chose the site and continues to use it is the indoor accommodations: the barn (dormitory style, sleeps between 100 and 125, depending on how friendly they are) and the cabins (of which there are four, suitable for holding between 2 and 10 people each).

Since HallowFest generally draws 250 attendees, tops, what this means in practice is that anyone who wants to sleep with a man-made roof over his or her head can. Some people do tent every year, and we get a couple of RVs, mostly from New Jersey and points west, but most Pagans, nature religion aside, are indoor people.

I stopped the van in front of the row of cabins. In the headlights they looked like miniature houses, all painted yellow. When I turned off the engine and killed the headlights the cabins and the rest of the campsite vanished.

I'd forgotten how dark the country was. I turned the

headlights back on, praying the van's antique battery would take the strain. Julian handed me the flashlight he'd been reading by without comment. I opened the door. It was like opening the refrigerator and looking in. I'd forgotten how *cold* the countryside got, too.

The lights went on in one of the cabins and the door opened. In the diffuse light of the headlights (fading fast, dammit), I saw that it was Maidjene.

Maidjene is about my height and makes Nero Wolfe look like a famine victim. She has long brown hair and a taste for flamboyant dress that makes her well-over-an-eighth-of-a-ton even more impossible to miss, and a lacerating sense of humor, as befits the originator of Niceness Wicca, the Wicca for people who find Mr. Rogers too confrontational. Tonight she was wearing a neon-striped caftan with an orange fake-fur robe over it and looked like a Day-Glo Obi-Wan Kenobi doll.

"Bast? It took you guys long enough. I thought you said you were getting up here before six," Maidjene said. I could tell by the broad vowels we'd woken her up; she's from someplace like Kentucky or Indiana originally and sometimes it catches her unawares.

"I didn't say A.M. or P.M. We got lost," I added feebly. Behind me, I heard Julian climb down out of his side of the van and come around to where I was. His glasses flared as the beam from my flashlight struck them and I flicked the light off.

Maidjene sighed. "Well, you might as well not have showed up if what you want is to set up; we can't get into the barn until tomorrow."

"What?" The Snake's table would be set up on the barn's second floor; I'd expected to spend the night there.

"Furnace broke last week. Heat's still off. Won't be on until tomorrow and even if Mrs. Cooper puts it on at six it's going to be *damn* cold in there unless I wanted to pay to have it turned on today, thank you very much, which

is extra, *which* I didn't," Maidjene said, more or less all
on one breath. "Why don't you all come on in?" She went
back inside her cabin, leaving the door open.

I got back into the van and turned off the lights before
the battery went completely dead and followed Julian (so
I presumed) into Maidjene's cabin.

The cabin smelled of dust and damp; the odd blank
smell of a place that people use but don't live in. The cabins at Paradise Lake are essentially single rooms, generally containing neither plumbing nor cooking facilities
and only rudimentary furniture. This particular one had
greenish wallpaper with a faded pattern of wreaths and
roses on it. I resisted the totally unwarranted temptation
to duck my head as I entered; the rooms are normal
height, even though this one seemed more crowded than
was strictly believable. It was filled with boxes and backpacks and groceries and duffel bags, suggesting that most
of Maidjene's coven was already here. Somewhere.

"They're next door, since why should anyone else have
to get the niceness up just because you and others of your
ilk are late?" Maidjene said, seeing me look around.
"Raven Kindred's coming, and Fred and Leigh and their
guys, and some people got here earlier: Fireflower Coven
from up to Boston and a bunch from Endless Circle, but
they're camping out. There's Diet Pepsi in the cooler, and
I think there's maybe some coffee in the thermos," she
added.

Coffee sounded good; I had the hollow watery feeling
in my bones that comes from late-night long-distance
drives, and I knew there was at least half an hour of shifting and hauling ahead before either Julian or I could
think of bed. I searched for the thermos while Maidjene
looked for her paperwork; we struck paydirt at about the
same time.

"Julian Fletcher, Karen Hightower," she muttered to
herself, checking off the names we use on our checks in

what is usually called the Real World. Our "real" names, though not by the yardstick most Pagans use. To Pagans and Witches, our real names are those we chose, for reasons of secrecy or sacrament, when we came to this place in our lives. It's always a minor shock to hear myself called "Karen." My name—my real name—is Bast.

And until now I hadn't known Julian's last name at all.

"Friday arrival, Saturday through Monday, Merchanting, Feast, Indoor, and Parking," Maidjene recited, confirming that we were intending to sell goods, were both participating in the Sunday Night "Feast" (the only meal HallowFest provides, and a logistical nightmare), required indoor accommodations, and needed parking. Every item had its own list, generated courtesy of Maidjene's computer.

I would not organize one of these festivals for dominion over all the kingdoms of the earth and real cash money besides. The picnic I helped Belle—that's Lady Bellflower, my former High Priestess—put on had been bad enough, and that was one day and local. I poured myself coffee into a clean mug I'd unearthed along with the Thermos. The coffee was still hot, but at this point I wouldn't have cared whether it was hot or not, so long as it wasn't decaf.

"License number?" Maidjene asked. I dug the paper I'd written it on out of a pocket and read it back to her. She made a note on yet another separate sheet, yawning.

"We were supposed to have the programs ready," she said, "but Bailey didn't get up here with them until late and they aren't collated yet. I'll give you your badges. Maybe sometime tomorrow," she added vaguely, referring, I hoped, to the programs.

Julian was standing in the corner by the door, keeping a wary eye on the piled clutter. He looked wildly out of place, assuming anything short of a Fundamentalist godshouter could be out of place at a Pagan festival. Julian is a Ceremonial Magician, which means that he is regimented, hierarchical, ascetic, disciplined, reasonably monotheistic, and 100 percent more organized (except when making road trips) than the average God-or-Goddess-worshiping NeoPagan. He is also, as you may have gathered, the oblivious focus of my unilateral sexual fantasies.

"So where are we going to sleep, if the barn's closed?" I said, when Julian didn't. Maidjene was digging through another pile of boxes with the patient late-night determination of a mole with a mission.

"So many kids this year, we're putting them in the barn in one of the big bunkrooms," Maidjene said, which wasn't exactly an answer.

"What joy," I said. The idea of trying to sleep in—or next to—a room full of children ranging from infant to ankle-biter, all with volume controls set at "Max" was not one that really excited me.

"You said we could have one of the cabins," Julian said. I turned around and stared at him. Maybe she had; Julian'd made all the arrangements having to do with the Snake.

"Well sure," Maidjene said, as if Julian were stating the obvious. "If we aren't using them for families with kids, *somebody's* got to be in them."

She came up with the box containing the badges and badgeholders and handed us two. I took mine, making myself the usual empty promise that I would fill my name in by the end of the weekend.

It didn't used to be like this. You didn't need to show a badge at a festival—just being there was proof enough that you had a right to be there. But that was before violence and gate-crashers of various stripes made it vitally necessary to know who belonged and who didn't. Now there are badges, and even something approaching security.

All forms of regimentation begin with an innocent desire for comfort.

"I'll just unlock the one on the end," Maidjene said,
"and you can put your stuff in there and then shift the
van on down to the parking lot." She handed me a plac-
ard to put in the van window to indicate that it, too, was
a member of the festival, and picked up a set of master
keys for the campsite that were attached to a Frisbee-
sized piece of pine with the campground's name on it.
"Here we go. I'll have it open in a minute."

"Do we get a key to the cabin, too?" Julian said.

Maidjene and I both stared at him blankly.

"So we can lock it?" he added.

The one last holdover from the Summer of Love in the
NeoPagan Community—at least at the smaller festivals—
is this: nobody worries particularly about keeping his
possessions under lock and key. None of the inside rooms
in the barn locked, and I'd never heard of anyone locking
the cabins—even the Registration cabin—during a HallowFest.

Of course, this attitude is tempered by enough reality
that most people still don't leave their wallets lying about
unattended, but the sense of community—real or imagined—keeps the pilfering to a minimum.

"You won't need to lock it," I told Julian. "This is his
first festival," I told Maidjene. Julian shrugged.

Maidjene led us down to the end of the row of cabins. It
was quiet enough that the crunch of my boots on the
gravel sounded loud and I could hear the sound that the
wind makes when it blows through pine branches. The
edge of the lake that gives Paradise Lake its name is just
behind the cabins, and the reeds around it rattled as the
wind passed through them. At a place and a time like this
it's easy to believe that the Earth is a living and caring
being.

"Are you coming or not?" Maidjene said from the door-way of the cabin she'd opened.

There was a bare bulb on a short chain, swinging slowly back and forth. The floor was a grungy green linoleum, flecked with white and yellow, and the walls were covered in a shrunken and aged paper patterned with yellow ducks carrying pink umbrellas on a pale blue background. There was a bare double mattress in a vinyl zip-bag lying in a corner.

"Okay?" said Maidjene. "See you in the morning." She wandered off again, keys jingling.

The cabin was about standard for HallowFest accom-modations; it had more or less what I would have gotten in one of the bunkrooms, more than I would have gotten upstairs, and had the advantage of being quieter and more private. There was a door in the back wall, and when I opened it I found that Maidjene had really done right by us: there was a rudimentary washroom tacked on to the back of this particular cabin. I turned the tap and was rewarded with a hesitant trickle of brown water, which meant that the toilet would almost certainly be working, too.

Despite this luxury, the lodgings were probably not up to a standard that Julian was used to.

I turned back to him. He had an odd smile on his face.

"All the comforts of home," he said neutrally.

I felt the usual awkwardness of being in a situation where one person—guess who?—has an emotional agenda and the other doesn't. "Welcome to the lap of na-ture," I said. "Let's get the stuff out of the van."

We could have left the stuff in the van for tomorrow, but there was no guarantee we'd be able to bring the van back up here then, and I was damned if I was going to take the chance of having to schlep all this stuff up from the park-ing lot. Unloading the van took a little bit longer than packing it had, and while we were doing that another band of lost travelers arrived in a white oversprung station wagon with Rhode Island plates. I discovered then that Maidjene's coven was manning registration in two-hour watches, since once Maidjene had squared the newcomers away and directed them to the meadow—where they could amuse themselves by trying to set up the tent they'd brought with them in the dark—Maidjene woke up Bailey and went to bed.

By that time I was on my last load out of the van. Julian had pulled his share of the weight but he had more of an interest in being able to find things again in the morning than I did. When I brought in the last box he'd already started unrolling bedding and had even set up what looked like a small folding tray-table.

"I'm going to run the van down to the parking lot. I'll be back in a few," I told Julian. He waved, absently, turning to another box. I closed the door carefully behind me.

The parking area is a not unreasonable distance from the barn and cabins, but the walk back up the sloping drive was an eerie thing at something after one in the morning. With all the lifting and carrying I wasn't cold anymore, and from a familiarity with the area I wasn't worried about marauding bears or bands of Kallikaks. This year Samhain fell near the full moon, which meant that now, three weeks earlier, the sky was dark. The stars were brilliant, the air was clear, and the scurrying sounds from the woods were raccoons at the largest, and more likely mice. Nothing to feel threatened by.

What I did feel was a sense of complete isolation; a sense that not only was there no human companionship immediately available, but that even the future possibility of human companionship had been somehow erased, as if everyone else had gone and left me alone here forever. Standing in the dark, on the road that led back up to the cabins, I knew I was actually not only in the middle of civilization, but five minutes' walk, at most, from several other people, some of whom were even awake.

And it changed nothing. I stood there and wondered what it would have been like to live in a time, not so very long ago, when the entire human race numbered less than a billionth of its present total and I might have walked for days without seeing any sign either of civilization or of people. I decided that New Yorkers prefer social isolation to real isolation and continued up the path.

When I got back to the cabin, Julian was brewing tea.

He'd been busy while I'd been gone. Several boxes had been piled together and a red cloth spread over them: on this makeshift table were a lit candle, a smoking brazier, and a mirror, as well as various other odds and ends including a small glass bottle half full of dark oil. The incense was strong enough almost to overpower the burnt-dust smell from the laboring ancient electric heater we'd brought along.

Julian had also set up the folding table that would go into the barn tomorrow, and along its seven-foot length were arranged a little kettle on a ring over a flaming spirit lamp, a Rockingham pot waiting for hot water, a tin of English biscuits, and two white mugs.

It was not an unreasonable amount of gear to travel with—I have friends in the Society for Creative Anachronism who bring not only tables, but chairs, bedsteads, and entire yurts to their camping events—but it was a level of domesticity I'd somehow never associated with Julian.

He had his back to me and was opening another box, out of which he lifted a teardrop-shaped pressed-glass decanter, its stopper made leakproof with wax, and two tiny matching glasses. Those he set on the tray-table. Then he turned.

"I thought something hot would be good," he said when he saw me.

"Where did you *get* all this stuff?" I said, meaning, mostly, the clever method of making hot water without electricity.

"From my lab." Julian smiled. "Alchemy."

Which was not unreasonable, considering Julian — if medieval alchemy (as distinct from its nineties offspring, spiritual alchemy) didn't work, he'd want to know exactly why not. Julian is a specialist in the theory and history of magic, and, in his own quiet way, a rigorous scientist.

I sat down on a stack of book boxes, which turned out to be a mistake. Sitting still made me realize how damned cold it was in here, and I knew from past experience that the heater would shut itself off long before the room began to be warm. The cold didn't seem to bother Julian at all.

I took my tea when it was ready and tried not to obsess on the pile of quilts and sleeping bags on the floor. The *single* pile. I'd been expecting to roll up in my sleeping bag in the barn — but then, I'd expected that the heat would be on there, too.

"I thought it would be warmer that way," Julian said neutrally. He was staring at the candle, not at the bed, and the mug of tea and the biscuit he was holding made him resemble an impoverished English vicar. If this was a pass, it was a damned indirect one — he might mean nothing more than what he'd said. I had a sudden passionate curiosity to know what he wore to bed.

"Yeah," I said. "Warmer."

Sometimes my savoir-faire amazes even me.

If Julian had been Valentino himself I would still have worn a T-shirt, sweatshirt, sweatpants, and two layers of wool socks to bed; there's no sense in being a damned fool about things and you try sleeping in an unheated cabin in Gotham County in the middle of October wearing anything less. I got first use of the bathroom, which might have been chivalry on Julian's part, except for the fact that this also meant that I got the bed first, and Julian's alchemical skills did not extend to conjuring electric blankets out of nothing. I curled into a fetal ball under the layer of sleeping bag and blanket and shivered, knowing I would be warm . . . someday.

Julian wore blue flannel pajamas to bed. Without socks. Ceremonial magicians are often ascetics.

He picked up the lit candle from the table and carried it with him across the room to turn out the lamp. He set it on the tray-table and picked up two full glasses that were sitting on the tray-table beside a tiny decanter. He handed one of the glasses to me. I sat up to take it.

"Skoal," Julian said, raising his glass.

It was syrupy-sweet and full of herbs—somebody's home-brewing—but as Julian'd drunk his, I followed suit. It was not the sort of vintage one allows to linger on the tongue; it had a nasty saccharine aftertaste, and one of the inclusions must have been *Capsicum*—red pepper to you—because I felt a rush of heat that went all the way to my toes as the liqueur hit my stomach. Warm at last, I burrowed under the covers again as Julian snuffed the candle with his fingertips and climbed in beside me.

Some time later—it couldn't have been more than an hour or two, as it was still too dark to see—I came bolt awake, the way you sometimes do out of violent dreams you don't afterward remember. The only light in the room was coming from the desperate coils of the electric heater, cycling on again before the Ice Age actually arrived. It made just enough light to see that Julian was not in the bed, but standing beside it.

I closed my eyes and prepared to go back to sleep. Julian got back under the quilt and put his hand on my shoulder.

The abrupt certainty of what I suddenly knew was about to happen jolted me with the pleasurable pain of an electric charge. I put my hand out and touched only skin, oiled with something spicy and ceremonial. The oil clung to my fingers. When he kissed me, the scent soaked into my skin. I could taste it.

I helped him push my sweatpants off. Neither of us spoke.

2

The next time I woke up, the light was stronger. My sweatpants were shoved down to the foot of the mattress and my sweatshirt was bunched under my head. Julian was sound asleep beside me.

I felt as though I'd been hit over the head, or had expected to die but been miraculously spared, or any number of things that paralyze the cognitive faculties. I slithered out from under the blankets, excruciatingly careful not to let cold air in, and gathered up my outdoor clothes by the thin wolf-light of false dawn.

I was so girlishly rattled that I even went outside to dress. Although it wasn't that much colder out than in, the cold air was as immediate as a blow to the heart, and I sucked air and hissed as I struggled into jeans and parka. There was a stump a little way toward the lake and I sat on it to pull on last night's socks and boots. By then I could distract myself with the romance of being up with the dawn, something I actually see oftener than I'd really like.

As the sun rises, it turns the sky first indigo, then blue. Any clouds take on a ridiculous set of Disney colors: purple, pink, yellow—even green. The tops of the trees, or mountains, or whatever's highest, go to full color, while the ground is still shades of gray. After that the stages of the process are much less distinct, with areas of light and color slowly equalizing until all of a sudden you realize it's not dawn, but morning.

It was still dawn when I walked down to the lake. The lake was covered with white mist in a low bank, blurring its boundaries. Across the lake and to my left I could see two dome tents, an orange one and a blue one, rising like strange giant mushrooms from the grass. The grass would be green later; right now it was still grayish with night and fog. Down here the air was even colder and wetter; I decided the lake hadn't been my destination.

I turned right, following the lake around to where it dwindled into marsh. There was a wooden bridge spanning the disconsolate brown sludge; it was slippery with rime as I crossed over it. Across the meadow, the trail began that led up the hill and through a scrap of pinewood to another open space. When HallowFest had the site nobody camped there.

I was panting by the time I reached it; there's a more gradual trail that starts behind the barn but I'd taken the direct route and it's a pretty steep climb. By the time I got there it was full day and I had no trouble avoiding the fire pit in the middle of the clearing.

The fire pit is about four feet across and a foot deep, lined with brick and edged with big white stones. The reason nobody camps here is that we use this site for the Saturday Night Opening Ritual and for the Bardic Circle and Bonfire.

I went over and looked at the fire pit. It was full of dead leaves, charcoal, condoms, and the odd beer bottle, but somebody would be coming up to clean it out and fill it with firewood later.

I'd relaxed as soon as I'd gotten here, and it didn't take much to figure out why: Julian wouldn't be easily able to find me here, should he conceivably be looking. It was an

irritating thought, and I couldn't face it right now; I hurried across the meadow and into the woods beyond as if
I were following a ball of string through a labyrinth.

The meadow with the Bardic Circle is at the edge of a
pine forest bordered on the west by the access road into
Paradise Lake and on the north by the houses that edge
Gotham County 6. The bulk of Paradise Lake's acres lie
east and south; this patch of woods is mostly a buffer
zone, leading nowhere. Once I reached the edge I'd have
to go back the way I came; due east out of the pine forest is a drop-off too steep for me or anyone else with
brains to shinny down.

I'd been walking fast, as if I had a destination in mind
where there wasn't one, and the part of me that wasn't
occupied in dithering had finally noticed that and was
just getting around to questioning it when I saw . . .

I could say its stillness caught my eye, but that would
be ridiculous: I was surrounded by rocks and trees and
neither one moves much. I could say it was the color, but
the colors were browns and blacks, just like the autumn
forest. I looked, basically, to reassure myself that it wasn't
what my mind was telling me it was.

But it was, and part of me wasn't surprised.

There was a man lying on his back on the ground. The
trees had kept me from seeing his hands and face until I
was right up on him; for the rest, he was wearing brown
corduroy pants and black shoes and a brown woolly coat.
It was an outside coat, a winter coat, and his left hand
was still in its glove. The right hand was curled among
the pine needles, waxy-pale and diminished. The nails
were blue.

I knelt beside him on the forest floor and pulled open
the unbuttoned coat. His eyes were closed and he might
have been asleep, but I've seen dead people before, and I
knew that he was dead, absent beyond any summoning
back. The coat felt heavy; when I lifted it open, a gun slid

out of the right-hand pocket and into the pine needles that covered the forest floor. It was, I decided tentatively, a .38 revolver. I didn't touch it. I hate guns. It comes of having had them pointed at me, I expect.

In life John Doe had probably been the upstate version of a redneck: fat, fair, and fiftysomething, clean shaven and closely barbered. He was wearing a red plaid flannel shirt and a white V-neck T-shirt. The only thing that didn't quite fit this picture was the aggressive gold crucifix bearing a muscular silver Jesus that he had around his neck. It was all of three inches long and he'd worn it on a heavy chain that would make it dangle about midchest. It was currently flung back over one shoulder and resting among the pine needles, as if it had flipped back when he fell. Only by looking very closely could you see the brownish spot, about the size of a quarter, on the front of the flannel shirt at about the place Jesus would have hung.

The shirt wasn't buttoned, which was odd. I pulled it open. There was a slightly larger spot on the none-too-clean T-shirt. The T-shirt wasn't tucked in, and a wedge of hairy bellyflesh showed at its hem. I eased the shirt up and looked.

In the middle of John Doe's chest, level with his nipples or a little below, was a weird puncture wound. It wasn't red and it wasn't bleeding; it was black and almost dry. A quarter, or a fifty-cent piece at the very most, would have covered it completely.

It wasn't a knife wound—which was to say, while he'd been stabbed, as far as I could tell, it was with something that made three half-inch slashes that came together at almost right angles, like the center of a Mercedes-Benz hood ornament, or a radiation trefoil, or a peace sign with the bottom center stroke removed.

I pulled the T-shirt back down, feeling sick. And then I felt even worse, because I realized that the fingers that had touched him to lift the T-shirt were oily. When I lifted them to my nose I could smell cinnamon, and when I looked at the dead man's face again, I could see that there was a shiny patch on his forehead, a little darker than his skin—but then, cinnamon anointing oil *is* a dark reddish-brown color.

The marks on his T-shirt that I'd taken for poor laundry skills became blotches of reddish oil applied to the skin and now soaking into the cloth. I found myself staring fixedly at the white drops of resin oozing from the trunk of the pine tree he lay beneath, and then my focus shifted and I could see droplets of hardened cream-colored candle wax upon the fallen needles on the forest floor.

No.

I stood up and backed away, tripped over my own feet and crashed sideways into a tree hard enough to knock the wind out of me. I'd hit my head, too; the pain made my eyes tear and stopped me from doing something stupid. This was not a time for stupidity.

There was a man lying dead in the forest, stabbed through the heart with . . . something.

And sometime before or after he'd died, someone had anointed him with oil and burned candles at his head and feet. And this had happened in a campground already being filled by one of the biggest gatherings of Pagans, Wiccans, and magicians on the entire East Coast.

I knelt beside the tree I'd run into and scrubbed my fingers dry in brown pine needles.

There are things that you do when you find a dead person, and one of the important ones is to tell the police.

I'm not one of those steely-eyed adventuresses out of prime-time fiction who stumbles through battle, murder, and sudden death without even mussing her hair, but by now I've had enough bad luck in my life that John Doe

didn't leave me really rattled for long. After all, he was
dead; how much more harm could he do?

The walk back helped, too. On the way I thought to
check my watch and realized it was barely six. I enter-
tained the craven notion of not mentioning what I'd seen
at all—it was entirely possible that no one else would go
up that way all weekend—and a small irrational part of
me was convinced that the whole thing was only a sick
practical joke that I was the victim of, and that when I led
someone else back up there, there'd be no one lying dead
among the pines at all.

I compromised with it by promising myself I'd tell
Maidjene. She ought to know, anyway, being the festival
coordinator. And then she could go with me and the police so that even if I was going to look silly, I'd have moral
support.

I tried the door of Registration. It wasn't locked. I
looked in and saw Bailey asleep in a pile of blankets,
looking like a giant hedgehog. I closed the door again and
went next door. The door there wasn't locked either.

It was warmer in this cabin than it was either outside
or in the cabin I'd shared with Julian, but then there were
eight people here, crammed into a space roughly twelve
feet by twelve. Fortunately, Maidjene was near the front.
I nudged her with my foot; there wasn't room to kneel.

"Wake up," I said, trying to keep my voice down. I kept
poking her until her eyes opened. She blinked, then focused.

"Come outside," I said. "There's a situation." I retraced
my steps over puppy-piled bodies and waited outside.
Maidjene and I have known each other for a long time,
even if she does live in Jersey. She joined me outside less
than five minutes later.

She hadn't bothered to undress from last night—rus-
tic conditions encourage the layered look—and looked
rumpled and wary and ready to be mad.

"It's six-oh-fucking-niceness-clock in the morning, Bast," she snarled in a stage whisper. "This had better be really exciting."

"How excited are you by a dead body in the woods up above the Bardic Circle?" I snapped back.

She stared at me; I could see she didn't believe it.

"There is a dead body in the woods," I repeated more patiently. "We need to call the police."

"You aren't making this up?" she said, after a long pause. I love the amount of trust I engender in my friends.

"No. I saw him. He's really dead. Where's a phone?"

Maidjene didn't move. "Who is it?" she said.

It hadn't actually occurred to me until this moment to wonder. "I don't know," I said slowly, thinking back. "I didn't recognize him. He was wearing a crucifix," I added, although that didn't automatically rule out his being an attendee of HallowFest.

And he'd been ritually murdered—both in the criminological sense and, possibly, in a magical sense. I thought about that and didn't say anything.

"Show me where it is," Maidjene said.

"Jesus fuck me gently with a chainsaw," Maidjene breathed reverently ten minutes later, staring at John Doe from a safe distance. She didn't need to get close to see he was there, and the police were not going to be best pleased by this becoming a high-traffic area. Because there really was a dead man at HallowFest, and now Maidjene had seen him too.

"We'd better tell Mrs. Cooper," Maidjene pronounced.

"We'd better call the police," I said.

In the end we had to do both, because although there was a pay phone on the outside of the barn, it didn't have a phone book. It only occurred to me later that I could just have dialed "Information," and later still that the reason for the lapse was that I felt like an outsider this far from

Manhattan and was looking for allies before I confronted the Establishment.

Helen Cooper owns and runs Paradise Lake and has been very tolerant of HallowFest's free-range hippie foibles over the years. She's a stout gray-haired lady somewhere in her seventies by now; she wasn't young even when we started coming here back in the early eighties. She lives year-round in the building at the entrance to the camp, a large rambling white clapboard house with a porch around three sides and a wooden sign out front that matches the one on the access road that says "Office."

It was a quarter of seven when she answered the door, and by then I'd gone back to feeling twitched, certain that at any moment somebody else would trip over the dead man.

I didn't think we'd wakened her, but Mrs. Cooper was still in her nightclothes. She looked at us through the old-fashioned green-painted wooden screen door. There was a silence. I realized Maidjene was letting me take the lead and hoped I looked more respectable than I felt.

"We need to use your phone. We have to call the police. There's a problem," I said.

"What kind of a problem?" Mrs. Cooper said.

I suppose subconsciously I expected everyone to know in advance; every time I had to explain it bothered me.

"There's a dead man up in your woods," I said, restraining myself from phrasing it "seems to be" with an effort. There was no seeming at all: there was a man and he was dead.

"Just a minute—I'll go up with you and check," Mrs. Cooper said, starting to close the door.

"Mrs. Cooper," I said sharply. I would have put my hand on the door but I'd have had to open the screen first. She stopped.

"I saw him too," Maidjene said.

"He really is dead," I said. "And we have to call the police now."

It turned out to be the Sheriff's Department that we called, not the police. Maidjene and I stood in the dining room while Mrs. Cooper punched the quick-dial number on her kitchen phone. She spoke to someone named John and confided to him that "some girls" staying at the campground "thought they'd seen" a dead body in the woods. She assured "John" that we'd be here when the car arrived.

"Car'll be here in about ten minutes," Mrs. Cooper said, coming back to the dining room. "I have to go get dressed. Would you like some coffee?"

I would, Maidjene wouldn't. Mrs. Cooper showed me where the coffee things were, and I doctored up a cup while Maidjene peered out the dining room window, for all the world as if she were Ma Barker waiting for the cops.

"This," she said, "is going to be trouble."

I shrugged. It'd already been trouble.

"I can see it now," she went on mournfully, " 'Human Sacrifice at Satanic Sabbat.' "

"Oh for gods' sake!" I snapped.

Maidjene turned back to me. Her face was set. "You know damned well that's what they're going to say, and nothing *we* say is going to stop another—"

"Witch hunt?" I suggested sarcastically. Maidjene snorted.

She was right, though, especially if . . . I stopped. There were too many variables to settle on one good paranoid conspiracy. Who was dead, and how had he died? Who had killed him, and why, and—

Mrs. Cooper got back about the time the sheriff's car pulled up in front of the house. There were two deputies in it. The driver got out and Mrs. Cooper was already opening the door before I realized the driver was a woman.

She was wearing a pale tan Stetson that made me think of Texas marshals, a light shirt and dark pants and the rest of the usual paraphernalia: black leather belt and a truly enormous gun. Her badge looked oddly common-place to me, and after a moment I realized why: Gotham County Sheriff's Office used a star-in-circle, just as Wic-cans did, only their star was solid and had "Deputy Sher-iff" written across it. She came inside and walked straight over to me.

"I'm Sergeant Pascoe," she said, holding out her hand. I shook hands with her; her grip was firm.

"This is the girl, Fayrene," Mrs. Cooper said.

"I'm—" I hesitated. "My friends call me Bast. Do you need my legal name?"

"Not if you haven't done anything wrong," Sergeant Pascoe said. "Do you think you can take us to what you saw, Bast?"

I must have looked panic-stricken; for a moment I wasn't sure I could find the place again. "There was a dead man," I said firmly. "Up in the pine forest above the"— I had to think a minute to remember the Paradise Lake name for it—"Upland Meadow. He really is dead," I said.

I must have sounded more frustrated than I realized; Fayrene put a hand on my arm. "Let's go see," she said.

"I'll stay here," Maidjene said firmly.

In the last few years I have found a dead body and barely escaped becoming one, but this time was different. Fayrene and I—and Deputy Twochuck, who drove this time—went by car back to the barn and up the road that led to the Upland Meadow site.

Deputy Twochuck looked maybe nineteen and kept staring in the mirror at me until Sergeant Pascoe asked him if he wanted to put the car in a ditch. That was how I found out his name was Renny. Renny and Fayrene, and their guns. I wondered how much trouble I was in.

They parked at the edge of the meadow; you couldn't take a car up into the pine forest even if you wanted to. Sergeant Pascoe got out and came back to let me out.

"You stay here, Renny. I'll call you if I need you." She turned to me. I pointed up the hill into the pines. Sergeant Pascoe sighed.

The body was still there.

It was more of a relief than I'd thought it would be; once I was sure it was there I stopped and leaned against one of the pines, catching my breath.

"Pretty worried, weren't you?" Sergeant Pascoe said.

"I thought . . ." I shrugged. "I don't know."

Sergeant Pascoe grunted and went to stand over the body, looking down.

"Anybody else been up here you know of?"

"I brought Maidjene up, but she didn't go any closer than this." I was standing about where she had been. "Somebody stabbed him," I said helpfully.

Sergeant Pascoe looked up at me from under the brim of her hat. She was blonde and had the color of eyes that often go with that shade of blonde, a steely sort of grayish-blue. I'd seen those eyes before in other faces. cop eyes.

"Now how would you know that?" she said.

"I . . . looked," I said finally.

"Sure you didn't do anything else?" She didn't wait for an answer. "Go on back down the hill and tell Renny I told him to call the M.E. And tell him to bring me up the tape."

I went on back down the hill and told Deputy Twochuck what Sergeant Pascoe had said. He gulped and looked excited, and picked up the radio mike and started spouting 10-codes into it. I went back up the hill.

"Hey! You can't go up there!" he said.

"So stop me," I said, walking off. Which wasn't fair to him, but it hadn't been a very fair morning, all things considered.

"Why don't you tell me what happened?" Fayrene said when I got back. John Doe still lay on the ground. It didn't look as if Sergeant Pascoe had touched him.

"I got here last night about midnight," I started, and told her everything that was any of her business. "So around dawn I decided to go for a walk."

"And what made you come up here?" Sergeant Pascoe said.

I shrugged. I wasn't really sure anymore. "It was in the same direction I'd been going."

"So then?" she said.

"Well, I thought I saw a body, so I went to make sure, and it was a body—"

"Anybody you know?"

I shook my head. "People look different when they're dead, but . . . no."

"And how is it you happened to take a closer look at our friend?" Sergeant Pascoe said.

"I just— I guess I just had to be sure."

It didn't sound like the truth, and for good reason— what I'd been making sure of was that John Doe hadn't just been murdered; he'd been sacrificed. And I had no intention of saying so. At least not yet.

About this time Twochuck made it up the hill, carrying a big bright yellow roll of tape. He stared down at John Doe and gulped.

"Fayrene, that's—"

"Why don't you go and cordon me off a nice big chunk of real estate, Renny, while we wait for the suits to show up?" Fayrene said.

Renny stopped himself with an effort. So he recognized

John Doe. That was interesting; about as interesting as the fact that Fayrene hadn't wanted him to tell me what he knew.

"Why don't you step back here with me," Fayrene said. We both backed away from the body, in the direction of the "Police Line: Do Not Cross" tape that Twochuck was stringing from tree to tree. We'd almost reached it when Maidjene and Mrs. Cooper got here. Either Maidjene had changed her mind about revisiting the scene or she was charitably keeping Mrs. Cooper company.

Mrs. Cooper was wearing green wellies and a black and red plaid jacket. She ducked right under the yellow tape and marched over to the body.

"Helen," Fayrene said. "You don't want to—"

It was too late. Mrs. Cooper stared down at John Doe.

"God damn," she said, as if passing sentence. She looked at Sergeant Pascoe. "That's Hellfire Harm."

Maidjene and I had both followed Mrs. Cooper.

"Jesus," said Maidjene, then: "Shit."

She'd been right. We were in trouble now.

Hellfire Harm—or as he was known to the HallowFest Community, "Jesus" Jackson Harm—had been a standing joke for years. He was a local character who'd sent long rambling letters to the *Tamerlane Gazette Advertiser* denouncing—among other things like vaccination, credit cards, and Suzanne Somers—our "unholy forgathering of Satanic Witches and Imps of Satan." These letters, which the paper resignedly printed in full on the editorial page, were written in a style that hadn't been much seen since Matthew Hopkins wrote his memoirs, and we'd used to read them out to each other over Sunday breakfast. While Harm had obviously been passionately serious, he'd just as obviously been several sandwiches shy of a picnic; a joke.

Not now.

"And you didn't know him?" Sergeant Pascoe said, looking at me.

We'd all gone back to the other side of the police line, and she'd sent Twochuck down to cordon off the path up from the meadow, too.

"No. If he's Jackson Harm, then I knew what he said about HallowFest, of course. But I only read about him in the papers."

And if he was Jackson Harm, the potential for publicity on this was, well . . . it'd probably make the city papers.

"Who killed him?" Maidjene demanded.

"That's an interesting question," Sergeant Pascoe said. About then two more marked cars joined hers at the bottom of the hill.

By New York City standards Reverend Harm got a lot of attention, but then, Gotham County probably didn't have as high a per capita homicide rate as my home turf did.

It was a learning experience. Fayrene, I discovered, didn't have the authority to pronounce Harm dead—that was left to the Medical Examiner. It took the M.E. about twenty seconds to confirm that the Reverend Harm was dead, probably from the stab wound, although he wasn't committing himself. The Crime Scene officer was hovering over his shoulder, waiting for him to finish. The photographer who had come with them was taking pictures of everything in sight, including the stab wound.

I wanted to ask what they thought could make a mark like that, but not as much as I didn't want to be noticed. Maidjene had already gone off with Renny—Fayrene wanted a complete list of everyone who'd been on-site between yesterday and this morning, and statements from them all. I wished her luck in getting them, or of getting any use out of them if she did get them.

The ambulance that would take Harm to the morgue arrived. By now the Bardic Circle was full of HallowFest attendees being kept from climbing the hill by three deputies in Stetsons.

Fayrene walked over to where I was watching the morgue attendants try to get their stretcher through the crowd.

"I guess we're going to need your name now," she told me. She'd gotten Maidjene's, and I imagine she already knew Mrs. Cooper's. "And you'll have to make a formal statement, but you can do that with Renny."

I nodded. It wouldn't be the first time.

I gave her my business card, wrote down my work and home numbers, showed her my driver's license, and even gave Lieutenant Hodiac as a character reference.

"You know Sam?" Fayrene said.

"Yeah." Well enough to mention his name and be pretty sure he'd remember me, anyway. Sam is Detective Lieutenant Samuel Hodiac, NYPD, Cult Crimes Division. Belle sometimes does advisory-type work for him, and besides, he saved my life once. "Some people I know do some consulting work for him sometimes." I was surprised she knew him, but then, the law enforcement community is probably as insular as the NeoPagan one.

"And you're one of those New York witches camping up here this weekend?"

There was no point in denying it. "Yes."

She sighed and shifted her weight. The leather belt she was wearing creaked.

"My boy Wyler's been bugging me to let him come up here and see what's going on ever since he heard about you folks last year." She sighed. "He's about sixteen, but he's getting to that age." At which, her tone implied, boys did not listen to their mothers, even if their mothers were heavily armed.

"Well, of course we wouldn't mind talking to him," I

began slowly, trying to channel what my ex–High Priestess Bellflower, community outreach maven, would say in
this situation. "But he *is* sixteen. He'd need his parents'
permission before he — "

"Came out here and danced naked by the light of the
moon?" she cracked.

"We don't do that," I said quickly, before I realized she
was joking. Sort of. She hadn't been serious, and the reason was obvious: if there was anyone in Gotham County
who knew exactly what we did at Paradise Lake, it'd be
the Gotham County Sheriff's Department.

"You've been to a HallowFest," I accused.

" 'Bout ten years back," she agreed.

That would have been the year that we'd gotten
deputies of our very own prowling the site at odd hours.
What they'd been looking for, none of us ever found out.

"So you know," I said.

About then the Medical Examiner left and two people
in plainclothes arrived. I was introduced to Detective
Lieutenant Tony Wayne and Ms. Reynalda Dahl of the
DA's office. They wandered off with Fayrene for a few minutes and came back alone.

"So what did you think when you tripped over that
body, Bast?" Lieutenant Wayne asked. He didn't look a
thing like Bruce Wayne, or even Val Kilmer. I decided to
forgot the obvious jokes. Detective Wayne was a solid,
dark-haired, ordinary-looking man with brown eyes, a
bushy mustache, and a gold shield. I wondered how much
ragging he got over his name, considering he worked in
Gotham County.

"I thought I should call the sheriff," I said. "He was
dead."

"You made sure of that," Ms. Dahl said. For a minute
I thought she was accusing me of the murder. She looked
formidably corporate; blacks storming the Establishment

bastions have to look whiter than white, especially in this field. It isn't fair, but then, what is?

"I looked under his shirt," I said. Even I could hear how defensive I sounded.

"Why?" Lieutenant Wayne asked.

"I don't *know!*" I said. "I came up here, I saw him—he looked *dead;* dead people look dead." I stopped and took a deep breath and tried to cooperate. I was innocent; cooperation was my job in the great civil machine. "I got down beside him and opened his coat. You could see the blood on his shirt; just a spot." I remembered something else. "He had a gun. I didn't touch it."

Dahl whipped off to say something to somebody else.

"It would ease our minds considerably if we could fingerprint you, Bast. Sometimes people touch things without noticing," Tony Wayne said. He was good; he had the kind of presence you would instinctively trust.

"Okay." I wondered if my prints were still on file down in the city. "Do I have to go down to your office?"

"We can do it here." He gave me a smile. Practiced charm. Soothing the probably innocent. "What happened after you saw the blood on his shirt?"

I thought back. "It wasn't buttoned," I remembered, surprised. "I don't remember whether it was tucked in. There was a spot on his T-shirt. Blood, you know? Shouldn't he have bled more?"

Lieutenant Wayne grunted; answering questions wasn't his department. Dahl came back.

"Crime Scene's got it. Smith & Wesson. Twenty-two."

In the words of Doonesbury's Uncle Duke: *"That thing wouldn't stop a hamster."*

"Something wrong?" Lieutenant Wayne asked me.

"I—" I said. "I don't like guns," I said feebly. Guns are a joke, until somebody points one at you. It wasn't so long ago that somebody had pointed one at me.

"So you saw he was stabbed," Lieutenant Wayne prompted me.

"He looked really dead," I said, knowing I sounded like an idiot and hating it. "I went looking for the police. It was about 6:30 when I looked at my watch."

"Helen's call was logged in at 6:55," Fayrene said. She'd come back without my noticing. "Her place is about twenty minutes' walk from here, cutting straight through."

"And dawn was around five today. That gives us a window of about ninety minutes. Are you planning to go anywhere?" Only this last was to me.

"When?" I asked blankly. I could tell the three of them thought it was funny. "I'm going to be up here through Monday," I said, nettled. "So are about three hundred other people from half a dozen states. Then we're all going to go home." *Please god.*

"Okay, that's about everything for now," Lieutenant Wayne said. "We'll be in touch if we need anything further. And we'd appreciate it if you didn't discuss this with anyone."

I nodded. Yeah, right.

"Come on." Fayrene took my arm. We went down the hill. Jackson Harm followed us down in a zipper bag.

There were a bunch of people, including Maidjene, standing around in the meadow.

"Sergeant Pascoe!" Maidjene called. Fayrene walked out to meet her.

"Look, are we going to be able to use this area for tonight?" Maidjene demanded, as soon as Fayrene was within hailing distance.

It was a reasonable question. There were cars parked on the grass, digging muddy ruts in it, and yellow tape was strung from tree to tree across the whole north side of it.

"You'll have to talk to Lieutenant Wayne about that," Fayrene said.

"The First Amendment—" Maidjene began argumentatively.

"Look, as long as we're on this side of the tape we're okay, right? And you guys are going to be gone by then, right?" I interrupted, desperately willing Maidjene to shut up.

"Nine o'clock?" Fayrene said, proving she knew as much about HallowFest as I'd thought. "Probably. Might be a deputy up there, though."

"That's okay," I said. Maidjene glared at me, betrayed.

"I'm glad," Fayrene said dryly. "Now if you'd all just clear out of here?"

I gave Maidjene the firm eye. She shrugged and walked back to the largest clump of watchers and started persuading them to leave for woods and pastures greener and fresh fields anew.

"It's like herding cats," Fayrene muttered.

"You don't know the half of it," I said. She looked at me, surprised I'd heard, I guess.

"So you don't think they're going to stay out of our hair?" she asked me.

It seemed to be a serious question, so I gave it serious thought. "I guess . . . a lot of us have too much confidence in our own abilities," I said.

She laughed. "I guess you do, but there shouldn't be much to mess up once we're done—and we photographed it all, anyway."

By now we'd reached her car. With two more cars behind it, it wasn't going anywhere soon. She opened the door and fumbled around in the glove box for a minute and pulled out a card.

"If you happen to remember anything else about this morning, you give us a call," Fayrene said. She wrote an-

other number on the back. "Any time." It was not a social request.

"Yeah," I said.

I was dismissed. Fayrene went back up the hill again.
I went off to help Maidjene clear the meadow.

It was about nine o'clock in the morning. The sky was
blue, the birds were singing, the sun was even warm. And
the Reverend Harm was dead, and public opinion—if
nothing more—was going to point to someone at HallowFest as his killer.

"The deputies would like everybody to clear out," I said to
a group of people I remembered faintly from other HallowFests. They were all in SCA garb of the later MGM period, and one of them was wearing a silver pentacle
brooch that must have been four inches across. NeoPaganism, as interpreted for these current Middle Ages.

"Tell them to leave us alone," the brooch-wearer said.
I wondered when I'd been appointed police liaison for
HallowFest.

"They better," one of the others said. I remembered
her. Tammy was what everyone called her; it was short
for Tamar. "Or Goddess'll zap them, just like she did
Jesus Jackson." She giggled, as if it were all a joke.

"Payback time," a man with a large hunting knife on
his belt agreed. I wondered what we must look like to the
forces of law and order: knife-wielding hippie freaks? Or
worse?

"They would like you guys to clear out of the meadow,"
I repeated. "Are you checked in yet?" I said on a sudden
inspiration.

It turned out they weren't; that got them moving. I
walked away quickly. It had been a stressful morning, and
people carrying on as if Jesus Jackson's murder were actually some sort of supernatural seal of approval on their
religion of choice did not improve my temper.

I gritted my teeth and went down the easy path to the barn, feeling like Cassandra booking passage on the *Titanic:* something awful was going to happen, and there was no way I could stop it.

3

I walked through the barn: you can go in one door and out the other to reach the cabins if you're in a hurry. Deputy Renny Twochuck had taken over one of the smaller rooms. The door was open, and there was a line of people waiting to make statements. I ducked inside. He raised his pen when he saw me.

"I've got some stuff to do," I said, "and they're supposed to get my prints. When shall I come back?"

He looked at his watch. "If you could report back here at 11:30, ma'am, that would be very helpful. And if you see"—he consulted his notes—"Mrs. Wagner, could you let her know we'll need her records?"

I nodded. There was no sense in embarking upon long explanations of why he wasn't going to get them, and fortunately I knew who he was talking about. Maidjene was Mrs. Wagner, at least until the divorce was final, but as for getting the attendance records for the festival, I could foresee a pointless tussle and the invocation of the ACLU. I wondered what I could do to head it off. Belle would be the person to ask, and she should be getting here sometime today. Lady Bellflower of the Wicca comes from a long line of union organizers and civil protesters and would be a better judge of our rights under the law than some coven lawyer who'd gotten his ideas about our legal rights from old *Perry Mason* reruns.

I bid the police presence a fond farewell as Deputy Two-chuck was explaining to someone, probably for what he felt was the ten millionth time, that he needed her *real* name, the one on her driver's license.

"That *is* my real name," Sparkle Starbuck said with ill-concealed triumph. "Here's my driver's license. See?"

I left before somebody asked me to take sides, and headed out the other door.

The HallowFest banner was hung over the door to the Registration cabin. It was after nine, and arrivals were starting to pick up. The space in the L-shape between the barn and the line of cabins looked like a cross between a kicked anthill and a madhouse: business as usual. There were some kids about toddler size running around underfoot while their parents checked in and unloaded. We call them our hereditaries, but I wonder myself if people who have had Craft handed to them without struggle will value it enough to cleave to it through all the betrayals and petty annoyances it contains. What view will they have of the Community, growing up in the middle of it? Will they see us too clearly—or not clearly enough?

Bailey was handling registration from a table underneath the banner. The murder was Topic A; I caught scraps of several conversations, some of which I fervently hoped the deputies would never hear.

"Do you know where Maidjene is?" he demanded when he saw me. "They want the registration lists and stuff, but I can't find them."

"They" being the Gotham County Sheriff's Department, and Bailey's excuse might or might not be the truth; Bailey is smarter than he looks. He's part Miwok Indian and resembles a shy hedgehog—a short one, which is apparently gods' curse on men, but Bailey doesn't act as if it bothers him too much.

"She was up at the meadow when I left, so she ought to be heading this way," I said, hoping I was telling the truth.

"I wish she'd get here!" Bailey wailed.

"Look, why don't you just give everybody badges now and sort out the registration later?" I said. He looked more grateful than the suggestion deserved, and I wondered what he knew that I didn't.

"Okay!" Bailey said, raising his voice and trying to sound authoritative. "Will everybody who doesn't have their badges please take them—and put them on? Everybody has to *wear* their HallowFest badge—"

I waved vaguely and headed for my cabin, feeling like a salmon swimming upstream. It was hard going. There were cars and vans and trucks pulled up haphazardly, blocking each other in, and people off-loading and generally catching up with one another since last year. An aura of high holiday seemed to suffuse everything and nobody much seemed to care about the inconvenience of it all.

Except me. I felt like the *memento mori* at an Elizabethan feast, certain that at any moment someone would notice I didn't belong here. It was a disturbing feeling, like waking up in the Twilight Zone. If I didn't belong here, where did I belong?

I was standing there feeling lost when a blue and white rental van pulled up, edging slowly through the crowd. I recognized the driver—and, by extension, most of the passengers.

Changing Coven had arrived at HallowFest. I abandoned my search for my own nametag and worked my way around to the passenger side. Belle slithered out the door just about the time I arrived.

Lady Bellflower of Changing Coven—to give her her full liturgical title—is short, round, blonde, motherly, professional, and (among other things) a very public Witch with a weekly radio show on WBAI. She's the woman who brought me in to the Craft and has run a Gardnerian-trad coven in New York City for the better part of fifteen years. She's been my closest friend for most of that time.

I looked at my watch. "You're late," I said. Not. It was all of ten A.M.—they must have left New York around dawn.

Belle shrugged and smiled. "So sue us," she said.

The others got out of the van. Sundance had been driving, of course, and Glitter, Beaner, The Cat, Dorje, and Actaeon—HallowFest veterans all—began unloading what was—as I knew from previous years—a pretty thoroughly stuffed vehicle.

"Topper and Coral should be here soon—they were coming up in their own car with the kids. Sallix had to work, and it's Ronin's weekend with the boys."

"Bummer." Ronin wouldn't dare jeopardize his visitation rights by bringing Ronnie and Seth to something like this. I caught Dorje's eye and waved. He waved back.

"So, how's it going this year so far? I heard Summerisle was running it, but now that Maidjene and Larry are splitting—"

"Summerisle's still running it, but there's been some differently-nice stuff coming down this weekend," I told Belle. It didn't take me long to fill her in on how I'd spent my morning.

"Is the Sheriff's Department being reasonable?" Belle asked. I told her about Sergeant Pascoe and Detective Wayne, and how they both seemed to be sane lawdogs with previous HallowFest experience.

"And they say we can have the Bardic Circle back by tonight so long as we keep out of the way now," I finished, "but they're asking everybody to make statements. I'm supposed to go do that as soon as I'm done setting up The Snake's table." I hesitated. "The Sheriff's Department wants to know the names and addresses of everyone at-

tending HallowFest this year, and I don't think Maidjene's real happy about that."

"Turning over her records? She shouldn't have to. I'll
talk to her," Belle said firmly. "And you keep out of
things," she added.

"Me?" I said, surprised. "I haven't done anything." And
I didn't want to, either.

"Well, don't," Belle said. "This is no time to be playing
'Lone Ranger of the Wicca.' The police can find out 'who-
dunit' without your help."

"I wasn't going to help," I said, nettled. "But—" It was
on the tip of my tongue to tell Belle about the candles and
oil, but something similar to prudence held me back.

"But nothing," Belle said firmly. "You aren't involved
this time: you never knew Reverend Harm; there's no
doubt that the murder's being properly investigated by
the proper authorities. There's nothing for you to do."

It was a sentiment with which I wanted desperately to
agree, but when I tried to something kept me silent.

"I don't want to borrow trouble," I finally managed.
Belle beamed.

"Where are you staying?" she asked.

I pointed to the cabin, hoping she wouldn't ask the obvious next question. And she didn't, bless the Lady, so I
didn't have to tell her that I was sharing the cabin with
Julian.

"You'd better go ahead and get set up," she said. "I'll
catch you later."

We went off in opposite directions. On the way back
to the cabin I saw Hallie of Keystone Coven (they're in
Pennsylvania, naturally) with an armful of the tie-dyed
ritual robes she was bringing for sale. I knew Hallie
slightly—she'd been in Changing when I first joined—but
she took Third and went off to found her own coven out
west almost immediately. I stopped her and we chatted—

the usual conversation of acquaintances meeting after long absence. Keystone Coven had already generated daughter and granddaughter covens, and I felt a guilty sense of promises unkept, as if I were being pushed to accept a responsibility I wasn't ready for. I pushed it aside, concentrating on immediate business—setting up the Snake's table.

Julian wasn't at the cabin, and his absence was almost as much of a relief as Jesus Jackson's body actually being present up there in the pine forest had been. What *was* in the cabin was the long table and all the boxes he and I had schlepped in from the van last night. Even though Merchanting wouldn't open until noon, there was no reason not to get set up before my date with Deputy Twochuck.

Renny Twochuck. And people ask why I prefer to be called Bast.

I found my badge and pinned it to my sweatshirt, then went into the tiny bathroom and yanked on the light. I turned both taps on full; eventually they'd run clear. Meanwhile I stared at my reflection in the blotched and unsilvering mirror, wondering how I appeared to the Gotham County Sheriff's Department.

Single white Witch. Thirtysomething, five-seven in socks. Figure not too bad, but better out of a parka, sweatshirt, and baggy jeans. Black hair, shoulder length, two months overdue for a cut. Blue eyes. Three holes in one ear, two in the other, all full of earrings. No visible tattoos. No makeup.

Nothing here to inspire a lot of confidence in the police mind, but on the other hand, I didn't look like a crazed killer.

I hoped.

What *had* put that hole in Jackson Harm?

Nobody here had any answers.

I dumped the parka and decided to change the ratty sweatshirt for a slightly more respectable sweater and a silk turtleneck (it has holes in both elbows, but it still looks fine under a pullover). When I pulled the sweatshirt off over my head I could smell bergamot, chypre, and cloves. Julian.

What had he meant? What had I done?

And what were the consequences?

I'm old enough that my first worry was that I might be pregnant—a worry that lasted exactly long enough for me to realize that I shouldn't worry about pregnancy as much as I should worry about infection. I thought I'd rather die than grill Julian on his sexual history until it occurred to me that the stakes were precisely that high— and that it was already too late to be safe.

The nineties are such a lovely decade.

There was nothing I could do about either possibility— pregnant or infected—right now except curse my stupidity and pray for luck—neither of which is ever as useful as a little forethought. Being in denial, however, works nearly as well. For a while.

I got to work, wishing I could have moved this stuff only once. The table was the worst; it was big and heavy, and awkward even folded, but I had help before I was even out the door with it—one of the Raven Kindred folks. Between me and Lew, we got the table through the crowd, into the barn, and up the stairs that led to the second floor.

As you may have gathered, the Paradise Lake barn is not exactly a barn, at least not anymore. It was remodeled many years ago, and now has two floors, for one thing (only the ground floor is heated), and a kitchenette, for another. It also contains two dorm rooms, each of which can bunk thirty or so, and four other rooms, which are set up with bunk beds to accommodate various numbers of people. The rooms were starting to fill with members of my tribe, my nation, my extended family: Pagans.

"Thanks, Lew," I said, when we'd got the table upstairs. The upstairs was freezing cold; the sunlight that made everything outside warm wouldn't make a dent in this cold air mass for some hours. If ever.

"Any time," Lew said. He was wearing a Thor's hammer on a thong around his neck. "You need any more help?"

"It's just boxes. You and Janna better grab some bunks before they're all gone."

"See you tonight then," Lew said. He waved and went off.

I picked out a nice corner space under the joists and near the door, with a window at my back. No one else was setting up yet, but it was just as well I hadn't counted on being able to bring the van up this morning. I went back for the first of the boxes. Soon enough I wasn't cold at all.

On one of my last trips back to the cabin—Julian was still nowhere to be seen and that was fine with me—a battered station wagon with Jersey plates pulled up outside of Registration, and a Klingon got out.

I'm a classicist myself, but this was a movies-and-new-series Klingon with the ridged forehead—latex, I was relieved to note. He was wearing what might very well have been a genuine Klingon Army uniform, for all I knew: he was the size of a refrigerator and I counted at least five knives before he made it to Registration.

"*Klash!*" Maidjene shrilled in a register only bats and dogs could hear as she ran out to meet him. Klash shouted something back; it sounded like a jammed gearbox.

I looked back at the station wagon. Five more people got out. They were all wearing fringed sashes. Some of them were wearing latex. One of the women—a little smaller than Maidjene, but not much—was wearing a leather corselet with brass cups about the size of baby moon hubcaps for the '57 Chevy of your choice. She bared her teeth at me and growled.

"Bast, I want you to meet Klash. Klash is the Orm of Coven Koloth. The HP?" Maidjene added, in case I didn't quite get it. She looked frayed but indomitably cheerful. I guessed she'd got back from dealing with Our Friends the Police; I didn't see Bailey.

*"Tlingan ko da jattle a?"** Klash said.

"Hi," I said. I resisted the impulse to see if my ears had suddenly stopped working.

"This is their first HallowFest," Maidjene said. I looked around. I was surrounded by Klingons. "I know them from Jersey."

"Can we, like, register now?" said one of the Klingons. Klash said something to him in what was, probably, Klingonese. Finally, the penny dropped.

"Klingon Wicca?" I said in disbelief. Maidjene winced.

"Some people call it that," Klash agreed, fortunately in English this time. He smiled. "Want to join the Imperial Race?"

"I have to finish setting up my table," I said, at the same time Maidjene said:

"I thought you could maybe show Klash and the guys around." *And keep them out of trouble,* her tone implied. Like any good hostess, Maidjene wanted everyone to have fun at her party.

Klash ripped off another sentence in Klingonese and made a sweeping gesture. Two of the Klingons shrugged.

"Ron says, we can help you with that if you want," one of them said.

---

*"Do you speak Klingon?"

"Sure," I said. It was as good a way to introduce them to HallowFest as any. "Come on."

The two Klingons followed me back to the cabin.

The NeoPagan Community was self-created to display an infinite tolerance for anything its members might do. As wiser heads than mine have pointed out, a community with no standards is no community, but, like science-fiction fandom and the bumblebee, the Community has survived infinite careful explanations of how it cannot possibly continue to work.

It is possible, however, that Klingon Wicca may be the bone of contention that breaks the camel's back.

While there are (my sources tell me) as many different approaches to it as to any other trad, and Klingon Wicca is only as accurate a label as, say, Norse Wicca is for Odinism, most Pagans understand Klingon Wicca to be a tradition of roughly Wiccan form and intention which takes its archetypes, mythos, and images from "Next Generation *Star Trek* Klingons — and, since there isn't all that much information available from the TV, they patch it together from a little Bushido here, a little Chivalry there until they've created a ritual and an identity.

What they've also created is a chasm between themselves and the majority of NeoPagans. Whatever else we say about ourselves, the one thing we all seem to agree on is that we are *reclaiming;* either the gods of our ancestors or the truth eternal; the path to perfect knowledge or the safety of the Earth. It is hard to maintain this belief when we see the same careful work and reconstruction put into something derived from a television show: How can we be serious if they are not? And how can *they* be serious?

They're not Pagans, say the Pagans, *they're fans.*

We're not fans, say the Klingons, *we believe.*

Where should the line be drawn?
Should the line be drawn?
And if here, then where else as well?

They guys' names were K-Rex and T'Davoth, I discovered shortly after they'd followed me off. They seemed more normal away from Klash ("His name's really Ron, but he doesn't like us to call him that," K-Rex explained), and willing to talk. It was a familiar story: they'd come to Paganism (however defined), as so many people do these days, after being exposed to it through SF. I wondered if they'd remain Klingons, or if the Imperial Race would become, in the end, merely another point of entry into our world.

With their help—"Strong backs, weak minds," T'Davoth boasted—I had the last of the boxes up to the second floor in two more trips. The cabin looked barren without them; all that was left was the mattress, my duffel bag, and Julian's things.

I told K-Rex and T'Davoth something about HallowFest, including the fact that the Sheriff's Department had found a body up on the hill this morning and wanted people to stay out of the area for a while.

"Cool," K-Rex said, which might mean almost anything.

I wanted to warn them that we didn't go in much for costumes, but that wouldn't have been entirely true. And ritual robes and Klingon battle-dress probably looked pretty much alike to outsiders, which seemed, at the time, to be a profound insight into the nature of reality. So what I did say was that I'd catch up with them after lunch to see if they had any more questions.

"Cool," said K-Rex again. T'Davoth nodded.

I didn't laugh at them. I didn't ask them their "real" names. Perhaps the actual example the Community tries to set isn't even tolerance so much as it is the freedom of allowing each person to define himself without discussion.

And maybe that won't work out either.

The guys went off to rejoin their Orm and I started unpacking the stock. I was the only one up here on the barn's second floor so far; it was peaceful and quiet, and provided the solitude I'd wanted this morning and never gotten. But what I'd wanted to use it for was lost just now. I worked instead.

Back in New York I'd taken the precaution of labeling the most important box in three-inch-high letters, so I had no trouble now in finding the cashbox (thirty dollars in ones and change-rolls), the tablecloth, the drape to cover the stock at night, and the credit card machine. After those things were on the table—and the top cover set somewhere I wouldn't bury it again, I hoped—I unfolded the two chairs and started in on the stock boxes. Fortunately I'd found the box-cutter early on, as Brianna had a free hand with a tape gun.

There was enough daylight coming in through the windows under the eaves for me to see; there are lights strung up here, but they're the pull-chain type and have to be turned on one by one, by hand, and it's a real pain. I knew the stock well enough to know what it looked like in the half dark, even if Julian had packed most of it.

So it was dark, and I was all the way back in the corner, away from the table bent over the box of jewelry, which was why the two of them didn't see me when they came in.

"I don't believe you had the nerve to come up here!" Maidjene said in a furious undertone.

"You're just lucky I did, now that one of your little buddies popped that fruitcake in the woods. You're lucky they haven't arrested you already, Philly."

"They didn't arrest me because I didn't kill anybody,

Larry," Maidjene said, deadly flat. I'd already recognized the voice. Larry Wagner, Maidjene's survivalist-fruitcake soon-to-be-ex-husband.

"That's more than you can say for your so-called friends. I've heard them talk about karma and holy wars — and Harm was one of those funny-mentalist Christians. He was stabbed, wasn't he? Everybody knows that one of those weenies you keep inviting over to our house did it."

Larry Wagner was an ordinary sort of pear-shaped whiteboy, with light brown hair that was starting to go and horn-rimmed glasses that'd probably wowed 'em in college. He had the sort of mouth that looked as if it spent most of its time in self-justification; not quite petulant but not exactly prim. He was dressed, as usual, as if he expected to be called to active military service at any moment: jungle-pattern camo parka, olive pants bloused into gleaming paratrooper boots, and black leather gloves. He was probably also carrying a gun: Larry loved concealed weapons and showed them off at every opportunity.

"The only 'weenie' I see here is you, Larry. Now fuck off."

"I'm not going to let you ruin your life over this, Philly. These people don't care about you. Once you come to your senses you'll thank me — I've seen you go through these crazes before; remember that time you had that crush on David Bowie? Religion is a tool of the government; everyone knows that — "

Larry didn't seem to have cashed too many Reality Checks lately, but that was nothing new, and listening to him call Maidjene "Philly" (not her real name) was starting to get on my nerves. I straightened up slowly and looked out the window. There was thirtysomething feet of Winnebago camper parked right outside the barn, snarling traffic even further. I recognized it: the infamous "Warwagon," named out of the Mack Bolan books and

Larry's pride and joy. One year somebody'd chalked *"Lasciate ogni speranza, voi ch'entrate"* on the side, and Larry left it there for most of a day until someone translated the Italian for him.

The Warwagon contained every form of paralegal radar detector and emergency band scanner known to man—at least it had used to—so I could take a pretty good guess that Larry's "sources" had been tuned to the sheriff's band. But were they really saying that *we* were responsible for Harm's death?

"Philly, all I want is for you to be happy," Larry was whining now. "When are you going to forget all this Wicca crap and come home? How are you going to manage on your own? You can't get a job—nobody's going to hire you the way you look." That was Larry all over, ever the gentleman. "Look, I'm sorry about your stupid book. If I'd known it meant so much to you—"

"You'd have done what you did anyway, seeing as it's just 'Wicca crap,'" Maidjene shot back with deadly mimicry.

"It's a stupid bunch of— You don't really *believe* that stuff, do you? If you stick around here, you're only going to get into real trouble this time!"

"Only if I kill someone," Maidjene said, in a voice that indicated it was a possibility.

"And I'd have to tell them that you people are anti-Christian—look, you come on home right now and that'll be that, okay? Nobody has to know anything," Larry wheedled.

"I've left you, asshole," Maidjene said, with frayed patience. "I have filed for divorce. We are separated. And I would rather starve in a ditch than ever have anything to do with you again. Okay?"

"Now look, Philly—" Larry began.

"You having problems, Jeannie?" a new voice said.

The newcomer was wearing a HallowFest T-shirt,

shorts, and Birkenstocks. Larry was dressed like Bizarro Rambo. Guess who looked more dangerous?

Ironshadow has a mundane name—I think it's Pat—but he's known through the SCA and the Community by the name he puts on his knives: Ironshadow. He stands about six-four and is old enough for his black hair to be liberally streaked with gray. He has a face that looks as if it's been remodeled several times on barroom floors, which is probably not too far from the facts. He's also a pussycat—if he likes you.

"I want you out of here," Maidjene snarled at Larry. "I want you out of this *state.*"

Larry smiled unpleasantly; I could hear it in his voice. "I've got my membership paid up. I'm staying right here. I'm entitled."

"I don't think you need to stay quite this close," Ironshadow rumbled. He has the deep bass voice that my new acquaintance Orm Klash had been trying to imitate. Larry looked at him.

"You've got to move your vehicle down to the RV parking, for one thing," Ironshadow went on, with scrupulous mildness, "and then you'd better go and register and get your badge, if you're staying. And after that I guess you better go tell the Sheriff's Department where you were when Harm was killed."

Larry made a faint stuttering noise in the back of his throat, as if he were trying to talk but couldn't remember his lines.

"And if you keep bothering Jeannie, I think you're probably going to run into a tree. Several times. So I'd be careful, if I were you," Ironshadow said solicitously.

To say that Larry flounced out in a huff might be crueler than necessary. There was a sad side to the little sitcom I'd just inadvertently witnessed: Maidjene had changed, Larry hadn't. And Larry wasn't accepting the inevitable consequences with anything approaching grace.

Which might have been unfair to Larry, but I didn't like him very well to begin with—he'd thought of HallowFest as his own Happy Hunting Ground for years and was notorious for hitting on the female attendees. I was glad Maidjene was dumping him.

"I don't know what to do." Maidjene was crying now. I felt guilty that I hadn't been the one to stop Larry and told myself that my arrival would only have raised the stakes of the confrontation.

"You'll do what you have to. You know that," Ironshadow said.

"Yeah. Well—Niceness Rules." Maidjene's voice was tired.

She turned and went down the stairs. Ironshadow followed her, but came back almost immediately with a suitcase. He must have left it on the steps before.

"You can come out now," he said to me.

I stepped from behind the joist and went over to hug him. It was about like hugging a tree: rock solid and full of energy. He hugged back, hard.

"I thought I saw you back there," he said after I caught my breath.

"I was setting up. I didn't want to interrupt them. But I would have if it got too nasty. Larry's such a weasel."

"He's got a few problems," Ironshadow agreed. "But not as many as the Reverend Harm seems to have gotten rid of."

" 'Marley was dead,' " I quoted, sourly.

"And you're the one who found him."

I nodded. It was hardly a secret, even if HallowFest weren't capable of fielding an Olympic-quality Gossip Team on five minutes' notice anyway. But Ironshadow didn't—gossip, at least.

"Look, 'shadow—if you wanted to kill a guy with a knife, how would you do it?"

He grinned. A short knife I hadn't seen a moment before appeared in his hand. Ironshadow throws knives as well as makes them.

I shook my head. "There wasn't any blood," I said, and heard the surprise in my voice. That was the thing that had bothered me all morning—had bothered me, in fact, from the moment I laid eyes on Hellfire Harm.

There was no blood.

"Then he didn't die by the blade," Ironshadow said. "Unless he was lying down when he got it. Standing up, even if you get him right through the pump, he's going to bleed for a couple seconds at least."

I nodded. Every mystery reader knows that. You bleed as long as your heart is pumping, or as long as gravity is draining the wound. There had been neither heartbeat nor gravity operating in the case of the Reverend Jackson Harm. There had been no blood anywhere around his body.

"Well, he *was* lying down," I said. "He was lying on his back." I went on to describe what I'd found as accurately as I could to the only person I could think of who might be able to answer my questions. I don't know how many of the tales Ironshadow tells on himself are true, but he's led a well-traveled life.

"Well, assuming he didn't get himself shot where you didn't see it, or overdosed on something," Ironshadow said, "assuming that what you saw killed him, then the only thing that fits is that the Reverend had to be stabbed while he was already lying down, and by somebody with one hell of a right arm on him."

"How come?" I asked, obligingly. Ironshadow snorted.

"You ever try to stab somebody through the heart, Bast? There's a lot of stuff in the way—bone and gristle and even muscle. You gotta grab 'em like this—"

Suddenly my back was to him and his arm was across my throat. I wrapped both hands about it as if I were going to chin myself. It was like grabbing one of the barn's cross-beams.

"—and then you gotta punch 'em *real hard.*" He tapped me lightly on the chest with his other fist, right about where the puncture had been on Harm.

"Or you aren't going to make it through all that," he finished, letting me go. "And getting there with an overhand blow from a kneeling position would be even harder."

I tried to imagine the choreography involved in that scenario and gave up. "Maybe he was asleep," I suggested dubiously.

But no. That theory required him to fall asleep—in the woods, in October, in street clothes—sleep through somebody half undressing him—neither his shirt nor T-shirt had been ripped, only stained—and continue to sleep while someone killed him with one powerful thrust to the heart.

"It doesn't make sense," I said.

"If it made sense, it wouldn't be Reality," Ironshadow said. "Look, watch this stuff for me a minute while I go get my table, okay?"

"Can I look through it?"

"Just don't break anything."

Ironshadow carries his stock in a battered suitcase. I laid it on its side and popped the latches. I lifted off the top layer of sponge padding and took a look. Ironshadow *athamés;* standard issue from Pagan Central Supply, most of them: six-inch double-edged blades with black lathe-turned hilts and your choice of decorator pommels: hematite, cloudy amber, even a quartz point. The union card for most Wiccans and their fellow travelers in the Earth Religions. There were a dozen of them; he might very well sell them all this weekend.

I lifted out the *athamés* and the sponge padding together and set them carefully aside. Next down was the expensive stuff, most of them probably special-order pieces being delivered here. One had a staghorn hilt with vaguely-familiar runes inlaid in silver and a blade so heavily greased that I knew it was iron, not steel; one had a rosewood hilt and enough jimping on the blade to make it look like fancy lacework. That one had a clear quartz marble slightly smaller than a Ping-Pong ball for a pommel-weight.

I coveted them both, mostly out of habit, while at the same time part of me was comparing every blade I saw to the mark on the late Reverend Harm and coming up empty.

There were a couple of other pieces — showpieces Ironshadow had little chance of selling here, but wondrous fair to look upon. I admired them all, taking my time.

The last item wasn't an *athamé* — or even a knife.

It had a short hilt of opalized bone that put it right out of my price range and the blade was a sickle-shape of pure copper that was already showing an oxidization rainbow.

"Four hundred," Ironshadow said, setting down a card table, a camp stool, and another suitcase. "It isn't spoken for."

I turned it over in my hands. A *boline*, the companion blade to the *athamé*. Traditionally a copper sickle, used to gather and prepare spell ingredients.

"Nice," I said wistfully, setting it back among its kindred.

"I could hold it for you," Ironshadow said.

"Hah." There was no way I could afford to drop four bills — my day job wasn't that dependable, and the outside freelance money I counted on to fill in the cracks had been scanty lately. I looked at the opalized bone glinting in the dim light of the barn.

"I'll think about it," I said.

* * *

I went back to work on The Snake's table and found that
Julian had been even more optimistic than Ironshadow
was—he'd packed two copies of *La Tesoraria.*

La Tesoraria del Oro is a nineteenth-century grimoire
drawing on a mixture of medieval French and Spanish
sources. It's a Christian-based series of rituals designed,
essentially, to obtain a bill of divorcement from God: to
sever all ties to the natural world in order to study that
world as a separate entity.

It had been my big freelance job last winter: every once
in a while, Tree of Wisdom has a spasm and goes into the
book publishing business, coming out with—usually—
some expensive limited-edition grimoire that no normal
occult publisher in his right mind would consider cost-
effective. And so I happened to know that in addition to
being freshly translated, typeset, proofread, and having
all its sigils and diagrams redrawn, *La Tesoraria* went for
about 250 dollars, hubbed spine, leather binding, sewn-
in bookmark, fancy endpapers, and all.

For those less daring, Tree of Wisdom produced a plain
hardback for 75 dollars, and we had one of those, too. I
said Julian was an optimist. He's also probably the only
person who'd actually have the patience to go through the
year's worth of rituals and nasty-minded asceticism that
the book demands and figure out a way around the joker
at the end: the impossible condition the magician has to
meet to complete the work.

Still, it's a pretty piece of bookmaking, even if it is—
while not exactly evil—just about the antithesis of what
I conceive Wicca to be. Still, it'd paid my rent when Houston Graphics hadn't. I set both copies out.

Merchanting was officially open by now; people started
drifting in. I sold a few things while I was still setting up.
I knew I should go and keep my appointment with the law,
but I didn't want to leave the table unattended while there

was a chance of the Snake turning a profit for the weekend. Goddess knew they needed to, from what I'd been hearing lately around the store.

It used to be that what you got at the Snake you couldn't get anywhere else, and so the shop scraped by, even with New York overheads. But today New Age is big business—Waldenbooks carries Tarot cards and shopping mall jewelry stores carry pentacles. And by undercutting the specialty store's prices, the mundane stores take away the profit margin that lets the specialty store carry the serious ritual magic supplies that the New Agers have no interest in.

And sooner or later, free market economics means no occultism at all, something I hope to put off as long as possible. Fortunately Julian showed up before one form of civic-mindedness won out over the other.

He went over to Ironshadow's table first. The knives were all laid out and glittering, making a pretty show in the sun. Ironshadow handed Julian one. Julian nodded, handed it back, and Ironshadow wrapped it. Money changed hands.

This was interesting—almost as interesting as my love life. Julian buying an Ironshadow blade? Julian's a Ceremonial Magician, not a Pagan. He considers most forms of polytheism to be beneath him. What would he want with an Ironshadow blade?

"Thanks for setting up," Julian said, coming around the table. "Why don't you come back at—five?—and take the cashbox and charge machine back to the van for the night. And maybe the jewelry."

"Julian," I said, "there is something we have to talk about."

He looked at me, waiting. I gritted my teeth and told myself I'd done harder things than this.

"About last night. I've got a clean blood test." I donate

regularly. "And you?" I kept my voice low; no one else was close enough to hear.

There. It was said, and it hadn't killed me. Now all I had to work on was my timing.

Julian smiled his detached plaster-saint smile, and I felt myself go hot all over. "Don't worry," he said. "You're safe. You're the first." He turned away and started rearranging the table I'd just arranged.

Julian was a virgin? An *ex*-virgin?

It was, I supposed, possible.

"Are you sure?" I asked, then heard what I'd said and wished I could be struck by lightning.

"Run along," Julian told me. "I didn't kill you."

But I would have been happy to kill someone—which made it fortunate, in a way, that my next date was with Deputy Twochuck. Not even I was self-absorbed enough to get in a sheriff's deputy's face out of season.

He started with my prints, which now made two law enforcement agencies they were on file with. Taking the print doesn't hurt. They roll your finger back and forth to get the whole image on the paper, resulting in ten square blotches on a stiff white form. It's kind of pretty, in a post-industrial way.

I was in the process of giving Renny a slightly more detailed account of myself starting at around noon yesterday when Sergeant Pascoe showed up. She had a carton of coffee in each hand.

"Don't say I never gave you anything," she told Renny, setting one down at his elbow. "And how are you?" she said to me.

As well as can be expected considering my sex life, I thought of saying. "Okay," I said instead. Cautiously.

"I asked Sam about you. He says you're a reasonable person." She pulled the lid off her cup and slugged the coffee back, letting the remark she'd just made lie there.

"I try to be," I said. "We don't want any trouble here." Platitudes "R" Us.

"Maybe you could fill in a little background for us, then. Bat wants to know. Tony," she amplified, seeing my face. "Lieutenant Wayne."

I suppose if your name were Wayne and you lived in Gotham County and were a cop your nickname would almost have to end up being "Bat." Geography is destiny.

"Okay," I said, still cautious.

"You done with her, Renny? Why don't we go for a walk?" Fayrene said.

Fayrene and I went for a walk.

"I thought maybe we could take a run down to the diner," she said. We were heading for the parking lot. "It's about the closest place around here to get coffee."

It was after noon; I realized that a cup of coffee at Mrs. Cooper's four hours earlier was no substitute for breakfast *and* lunch.

"Fine." And then whatever she wanted to say—or have me do—could take place in decent privacy. "You wouldn't know any place around here that does Chinese?"

She didn't. We ended up at a place called Mom's, a diner just up County 6 that was a retro vision in brushed aluminum and gold-flecked white Formica. I ordered coffee, lots of coffee, and the double bacon cheeseburger platter deluxe, figuring dinner was only a remote possibility.

"Now, Sergeant Pascoe, what is it I can do for you?" I asked, taking the war to the enemy, as the saying goes.

"You might as well call me Fayrene," she said. "There isn't enough space in the office I've got for my name and a title, too. And you go by Bast?"

"Most of the time." Ray at my workplace, Houston Graphics, calls me Kitty—either because it's short for "Miss Kitty" (Ray's a fan of TV Westerns) or because Bast is the Egyptian goddess of cats—but that's about it for theme and variations.

"Well, Bast, first of all you can convince your friend in the orange dress"—that was Maidjene—"to find her records of who's supposed to be camping at Paradise Lake this weekend, because if we don't get them, we just might have to decide to hold her as a material witness." Fayrene frowned at me.

A material witness, in case you didn't know, is just like a criminal, except with fewer civil rights—like arraignment, representation, and the chance of seeing the outside of the local jail before Hell freezes rock-solid.

"Uh-huh," I said. "What are you going to do with them? Are you going to make them public?"

"Now why should we do that?" Fayrene said back.

I hadn't the faintest idea. "It's just that people get jumpy, having information about them turned over to government agencies." Considering what a lot of it ends up getting used for. I wondered what the grounds for Maidjene and Larry's divorce were, and which of them was officially bringing suit, and whose files that information would sit in until the end of time. "If you could tell me what you want it for . . ."

"We want it to catch whoever stuck Hellfire—if that's all right with you," Fayrene said, starting to sound annoyed.

"But it won't," I said. "Not if you think it's going to tell you who's at the festival or when they got here."

I launched into Basic Explanation #71, about how anyone can call himself a Pagan—or a Witch—without reference to any accrediting agency whatsoever, and about how the forms the registrants send into HallowFest every year are generally for entertainment purposes only.

"Some people got here yesterday and went to the site—and of those, some told Maidjene they were here, and some haven't gotten around to it yet. Some got as far as the area last night and checked into a local hotel instead of going to the site." There are some around here, unlikely as that seems. "Some are getting here today. Some even live around here—well, sort of—and usually they put some people up, if they're coming from a long way away. But you can't tell from the forms. Some people just show up, because they've come every year."

"We'll just have to do our best without crystal balls and Tarot cards," Fayrene said sardonically. "And *with* the membership list. Consider yourself deputized."

I wasn't sure whether she could do that or not—and if she could, I'd prefer that she do it to somebody a lot more trustworthy.

And if she did, I at least wanted to get a badge out of it.

"I'll talk to Maidjene," I said. I wondered if I was going to have either a reputation or a nervous system left by Monday. "Do you think you're going to catch . . . whoever it was?"

"Well, we like to think so. Body's down to the morgue; we should know more by Monday."

"Like how whoever it was got him to lie down and strip?" I asked, ever helpful.

The waitress arrived, bringing my hamburger platter and a piece of pie for Fayrene.

"Go on," Fayrene said neutrally.

I explained my guesses, in between bites of burger. I left Ironshadow's help out of my story, but told Fayrene everything else, including things she probably already knew, like how strong the killer would have to be—and how lucky. "So who got Harm to hold still?" I finished.

And, I suddenly wondered, what had both of them— Harm and the murderer—been doing up there in the first place?

" 'How' is what you ought to be asking," Fayrene corrected my "who." "And we won't know that until sometime next week."

By which time everyone on the site would be gone.

"Anybody out there we should talk to?" she went on. "Maybe somebody with a really short temper? It can't be any secret to you folks that you weren't exactly Harm's favorite people."

"Nobody from HallowFest would do something like that," I said indignantly.

"Someone did," Fayrene said dryly, "or do you think our local boys light candles around people and slop them all over with perfume before they stab them?"

It took a moment for what she'd said to sink in. Then I closed my eyes and tried to keep my burger where it was.

"Hi, Mom," a gangling young local said.

4

J eff said you'd 10-70'd in from here. Did you know that
old Hellfire got himself murdered up with the
Witches? Mom, can I go on up there, and—"

"What are you doing out of school this time of day?"
Fayrene demanded, then apparently gave up the question
as a bad job and said, "Bast, I'd like you to meet my son
Wyler."

Wyler Pascoe was sixteen years old, an only child (as
I found out later), and blond like his mother. He seemed
likeable enough, which was a good thing, as it had apparently never occurred to Wyler Pascoe in all his young
life that anyone wouldn't want him around.

"We had a half day today; I got out at noon," Wyler
protested, all hurt innocence. He stared at me.

"Hi, Wyler. My name is Bast."

He took this as an invitation to sit down without oth-
erwise acknowledging my presence; I moved over to make
room for him.

"Hi. Mom, can I go up there and see them? I don't have
to be at the garage until 3:00, and Felix doesn't like it if
I show up early, and I *did* only have a half day, so I
thought—"

I don't have much experience with teenagers, but my

experience, they only talk that much and that fast when they are trying to put something over on their parents.

"No," said his mother. "Paradise Lake is private property."

"But Mrs. Cooper won't mind—she lets me go up there all the time, and—"

"But the Witches *would* mind. Wouldn't you?" Fayrene said to me.

Wyler seemed to really notice I was there for the first time. He stared at me, goggle-eyed and silent.

I welcomed the distraction from Fayrene's last bombshell, even if the list of things I was ignoring to concentrate on the present moment was starting to get ridiculously long.

"You're one of the Witches?" Wyler breathed in awe. "A real Witch?" He stopped, and I gave him points for not asking what usually turns out to be the next question, which is whether I can turn the speaker into a toad. My stock response is that I don't believe in improving upon Nature's handiwork.

"That's right," I said. "Wicca is a NeoPagan religion. There are a lot of different NeoPagan traditions represented at HallowFest this weekend." Belle would be proud of me. "And a lot of families bring their kids, too." Let's hear it for family values.

"So can I go?" Wyler demanded again. "I won't be long."

Fayrene frowned. I thought it best to be diplomatic.

"You'd have to have bought a membership several months ago—they don't sell them at the door." Which is different from paying at the door for something you reserved several months ago, and whoever was running it each year tried not to do that either. Besides that, we don't sell memberships to anyone under eighteen unless their parents are attending too, but there wasn't any point in mentioning that.

"Oh." There was a pause while Wyler digested these

facts and Fayrene relaxed. "Can I have your french fries if you don't want them?"

I didn't want the french fries, I didn't want to be here, and most of all I didn't want to be the Sheriff's Office liaison to HallowFest. It didn't look like I was going to get what I wanted, except maybe with regard to the fries.

"Wyler, leave the lady alone," Fayrene said.

"Have them," I said, pushing my plate toward him.

"Is she the one that whacked him?" Wyler said, around a mouthful of fries. Fayrene snorted.

"Who would want to see Jackson Harm dead?" I asked, trying to ask detective-questions in the best amateur tradition.

"Other than everybody?" Fayrene said.

There was a pause while Wyler finished my fries, remembered somewhere else he had to be, and left. I drank coffee and tried not to panic. John Law thought Harm's was a ritual murder on a site full of ritualists.

"You knew, didn't you?" Fayrene said, when we were alone again.

"I saw the wax on the pine needles, and I knew there was anointing oil on the body," I admitted. I saw Fayrene's eyes flash and hurried on. "But I'm not a cop—a sheriff's deputy, I mean—and I didn't want to jump to any conclusions and tell you your job."

"You were just going to keep quiet and hope we'd miss it?" she said. Cops have this trick they do with their voices; the words sound like they're just making conversation, but the inflection they give things makes them sound as if they can mean anything at all. Or nothing.

I took a deep breath.

"I wasn't going to mention it because I couldn't see how my guesses could do you any good. And because I could be wrong. And because if there were really something to see, you'd spot it." And because I'd been praying I was wrong, but I didn't say that. I didn't have to.

"Well, suppose you start guessing now," Fayrene said, not letting me off the hook.

"About who killed Jackson Harm?" I asked, barely keeping the outrage out of my voice. "I don't even know for sure how he was killed—or when."

"Cautious type, aren't you?" she said, scowling. "Welladay, let's see. Unless he was poisoned, that pop through the heart was how he got it. As for when, I'm not the coroner, but rigor had passed off by the time we got to him, and the night was cold—which would delay both onset and release—so say somewhere between midnight and four A.M. Maybe as late as five, though—bodies are funny that way."

"Why are you telling me this?" I asked mournfully.

"Because you want to help us," Fayrene said, grinning with a shark-mouth full of teeth.

I supposed I did, once you defined enlightened self-interest loosely enough. I got back to the site about an hour later, armed with a mandate from the Sheriff's Office to do what I could to help—which boiled down to acting as a translator, mostly.

And to get Maidjene to turn loose of the Festival records.

I didn't see the Warwagon when I got back to the barn, so it looked as if Larry'd followed Ironshadow's, um, advice. There was a copy of the HallowFest schedule written out large and posted on the bulletin board on the side of the barn. Right now I had a choice between Woman's Herbalism of the Northeast (outside), Introduction to the Lesser Banishing Ritual (barn, upstairs, at the opposite end from the merchants), and Mediation for Coven Leaders (barn, downstairs). The herbalism workshop noted that its location had been changed from the Bardic Circle to the Lake Meadow. I noted the times for the Opening Ritual and Bardic Circle this evening.

There was a sign saying that Hoodoo Lunchbox would be playing at the Circle, and I was glad to see that Xharina had decided to make it up here. Then I thought things over and decided I actually wouldn't really wish this weekend on anyone I liked.

I tracked down Maidjene at the herbalism workshop after drawing a blank at both of the others. It was being held in an open space on the tenting field on the far side of the lake. The women were gathered in a circle around a gray-haired woman in her sixties who was wearing a crown of autumn leaves on her head. Fortunately, Maidjene was on the outer edge. I knelt down beside her.

"I need to talk to you," I said, keeping my voice down.

"Now?" Maidjene said.

"Now would be good," I said back.

The workshop leader was explaining that pennyroyal was no substitute for legal and political control of our reproductive rights—among other things, pennyroyal is an abortifacient, and damned dangerous when used for that purpose—and passing out flyers with addresses of various national politicos. Maidjene and I both took one, and then she stood up. I followed her.

She headed back in the direction of the cabins, but stopped on the bridge and stared down into the brack.

"You've got to give the police those records," I said. There was no point in being subtle.

"I don't have them," Maidjene said. She couldn't quite keep the smugness out of her voice.

"Find them. Look, Maidjene, they don't care about us. All they want is their killer."

"And they want to look for their suspect in the HallowFest registration forms. Forget it. Niceness Rules. I talked to Belle. I'll get a lawyer."

"You'll lose."

"Thank you very niceness much for the vote of confidence, Bast."

"They will arrest your niceness *tuchis*, Maidjene."

"I don't care. They're picking on us because we're different, Bast, and because we make good scapegoats."

"They'd ask anybody for this stuff!" I pointed out, getting exasperated. "The New Baptist Republicans, even."

"Sure." Maidjene looked tired. "But the New Baptist Republicans wouldn't get harassed out of their job once it got back that they'd spent the weekend having hot sex and Satanic drug orgies in Upstate New York." Her shoulders sagged. She looked every year of her age plus ten or so more.

"You should get out of your ivory tower more, Bast. It isn't like it was in the sixties," Maidjene—who was my age and thus too young to really remember them—said. "It isn't even like it was in the eighties. The hammer's coming down. And if you aren't right in the mainstream, you're going to get smashed. It's already starting: conform, don't make trouble, don't *need* anything—do you know what they're doing to the entitlement programs in Congress? I can't give the police those records. Not because of what they'll do with them now; but what about five years from now? What about then?"

Like many of us, Maidjene has slightly left-leaning views: most members of a racial/religious/sexual/political minority get radicalized early and often. I wanted to tell her she was crazy, but lying well is not one of my strong suits.

"Sergeant Pascoe said they'd keep it quiet," I offered feebly. "They only want to catch the killer."

" 'Love work, hate mastery, and seek no friendships among the ruling class,' " Maidjene said, misquoting Hillel ben Shahar slightly.

"Maidjene, have you really thought this through?"

"If they ask me, I'm going to have to tell them I don't have the records," she repeated stubbornly.

If she were actually telling the truth, HallowFest would be wiped out financially—next year's organizers wouldn't be able to tell who'd paid, or who to send registration forms to. Not to mention that we were probably going to lose this site anyway, records or no.

But if Maidjene were telling the *literal* truth, as elves and Witches often do, someone else might have the information the Sheriff's Office wanted.

"Try to see your way clear to helping them," I said. "Or else whoever's trying to make trouble for us gets what he wanted." I barely remembered in time that she didn't know that Harm had been anointed before he was stabbed, or about the candles. And I didn't see any reason to share that information, now or ever.

"You don't understand, Bast," Maidjene said. "This isn't just something I do on weekends. This is my *life.* I'm not going to say 'Oh, it just doesn't matter' any time it's more convenient to cooperate. I don't have a right to give up that list, even if somebody else in my situation was to feel differently."

Wicca wasn't a weekend thing for me any more than it was for Maidjene, and sometimes it was hard to count the friends and potential friends I'd lost to the choices I'd made. I thought she was wrong, but I didn't think I could change her mind. The martyr's crown bespells those of us who aren't Christians, too.

"Okay," I said, backing off. "I just thought I'd tell you."

"Sure." Maidjene smiled wanly. "May the Nice Be With You. And if anybody shows up waving a bloody knife, I'll point him in your direction."

"Do that," I said. She went back to the workshop. I crossed the bridge in the direction of the barn.

* * *

It would be really nice if the killer confessed—and turned out to be a local boy totally unrelated to HallowFest who'd popped Harm for totally mundane motives.

Unfortunately, a theory like that didn't wash. It couldn't. Harm had been killed right in our back yard, in a fashion that deserved at least a paragraph in "America's Unsolved Mysteries," by someone who used at least some of the bells and whistles of our practices. This left only three possibilities:

1) It was a religiously-motivated ritual murder by one of our HallowFest Pagans. This one was pretty hard to believe. Human sacrifice is the stuff of lurid rumor and afternoon talk shows, not reality. Certainly the occult tradition holds that there is power innate in spilled blood, and some of the older grimoires—like the *Tesoraria*—talk about ritual murder, but only as a symbol. It's a long way from theory and tradition to cold steel in the night. And a degree of religious faith ardent enough to encompass human sacrifice was something I didn't think I could find in Vatican City, let alone at Paradise Lake.

2) It was a secularly-motivated killing of Harm by one of us tricked up to look like a ritual murder. There wasn't much reason for this either, unless the killer was already preparing an insanity defense. I supposed I could come up with a real-world motive sooner or later if I tried, though—not that it would be up to me. The problem with this idea was that none of us was really local—except for HallowFest, we really didn't have much chance to rub up against Jesus Jackson Harm.

3) It was a murder by a non-Pagan local who was attempting to frame someone—anyone—at HallowFest for it. It might be mere chauvinism, but I liked this idea much better than either of the others. It had a lot of built-in flex, including the fact that I didn't have to worry about a motive—hadn't Fayrene said everyone hated Harm? And we had written indication of how much he'd hated us.

Enough to die a martyr's death, secure in the glorious resurrection to come, just to cause us trouble?

Maybe. Or maybe he'd been an unwilling sacrifice.

Mindful of my might-be deputization, my next stop was the Registration cabin. One of Maidjene's other coveners, a woman I knew as Sabine, was there to direct newcomers in the right directions. She had a sheet of paper in front of her and was copying out Sunday's schedule for posting. There were a pile of parking permits and a box of name tags on the table and no other paperwork in sight. A boombox in the background was playing a Charlie Murphy tape. She handed me a copy of the program (collated at last).

"So what are you doing about registration?" I asked, stuffing the program into a pocket.

"Oh, we're just giving badges to everybody. It'll be okay. I guess they'll send out next year's mailing from last year's list."

Not that they'd have to, I realized, unless the Sheriff's Office got the bright idea of subpoenaing Maidjene's hard disk from her home computer. HallowFest had a high-tech backup for those well-and-truly-sought-after registration forms.

"So what'd she do with the paperwork?" I asked, hoping the question sounded harmless.

"Over there," Sabine said. "We're going to burn them tonight at the fire." She sounded so unconcerned that I wondered if I was the only one here who had all my marbles—or, at least, a different set than were in general issue. "Hey, are you the one that found that guy's body?"

"Yeah." I looked at the box. I knew what I was thinking and I hated myself for thinking it.

"Isn't it great? I mean, not that he's dead"—Sabine didn't sound especially sincere—"but that *they're* finally getting some of what happened to *us.*"

There is a mythology still current in the NeoPagan Community—and immortalized in popular song—that during the "Burning Times" (roughly four centuries, beginning with Dame Janet Kyteler in 1324 and ending around the end of the eighteenth century) nine million European women were burned for the "sin" of "witchcraft."

In addition to smacking unpleasantly of one-upmanship on this century's better documented holocaust, it isn't true: there weren't nine million of them and they weren't burned. And of the several hundred thousand who did die by the rope, the rack, and even the stake, most were Jews, heretics, and the mentally ill. Of course, there may even have been a few Witches among them, but I like to think they wouldn't approve of their deaths being used as an excuse for moral insensibility by their spiritual descendants.

"That doesn't make it right," I said. My voice was hoarser than I liked to hear it.

She looked at me, her expression of satisfaction fading into something like alarm. Belle tells me I have no tact, and after all these years I'm beginning to suspect she's right. I did what I could to repair matters.

"Look, do you want me to cover for you here? It looks like there isn't much to do, and I'm not too interested in this set of workshops."

"Just about everybody's here," she agreed. "But maybe you could do, like, from three to five? Lorne was supposed to, but he's got to go to town for a firewood run, on account of we couldn't get up there this morning."

"Yeah, sure," I said, not looking at the box again. It had a Kinko's logo on the side, and was the kind that holds a thousand #10 envelopes. It was taped up, and tied with ribbons like a Christmas package.

"I'll check with Maidjene, but thanks for asking at least," Sabine said. "Look, I'm sorry if that guy was, like, a friend of yours."

"Oh, no." Some of my best friends, as the saying goes, but that didn't include the Reverend Jackson Harm, and if I'd only read about his death in the paper I would probably have had something like Sabine's reaction, if only in the privacy of my own mind. "It's okay."

But it wasn't. Only understandable.

I went back to the cabin, feeling like I was going in circles in more ways than the obvious. My palms were sweating, and I could still taste the burger I'd had for lunch, unhappy in its new home.

I like to think that it wouldn't have occurred to me if the box hadn't already been wrapped and tied like a virgin sacrifice. But if Maidjene was going to burn the records anyway, couldn't they just . . . disappear without anyone knowing?

And then the deputies would stop asking about them, and Maidjene wouldn't be arrested, and everything would be fine.

Right?

I knew what I planned to do and I hated myself. I was going to do my best to steal the HallowFest registrations before Maidjene burned them and turn them over to the police, unless something happened to stop me.

Why?

Because it was the lesser of two evils? Because it would save Maidjene from further hurt at a time she needed it least? Or was I just kidding myself? Maybe I was looking for a martyr's crown, too.

I soothed my conscience by telling it there was no way Maidjene would take Sabine up on my offer to baby-sit after our conversation this morning. I told myself that even if she did, I wouldn't be able to get into the box. And as I was telling myself that, I was loading the inside pockets of my parka with enough copies of the Tree of Wisdom mail-order catalogue to equal the weight of what I hoped to steal, and a box-cutter and a tape roll to camouflage my theft.

Now that the long table and the boxes were gone, Julian's altar was set up on the folding tray-table he'd brought up. I looked down at my face in Julian's mirror. *Oh, Goddess, don't let me fuck up,* I pleaded silently. *Let this be the right thing to do. Let my brains not have turned to Wheatena. And while You're at it, let me find out who the killer is so I don't have to do this at all.*

There was no answer, not that I was expecting one. But the air was charged with the *numen* I associate with good ritual. She was present, and She was listening, and I was acting in accordance with Her will.

I tell myself.

The door to the cabin slammed open.

"Bast! Come quick!" Maidjene bawled.

I bailed out the door of the cabin and followed Maidjene in the direction of Mrs. Cooper's house. I could hear her gasping as she ran; she wouldn't have enough breath left over to answer questions.

She didn't have to.

There was a crowd gathered in front of Mrs. Cooper's house. I heard them before I saw them. Maybe twenty people, a few of them ours. I saw Orm Klash, and a man named Ragnar, who I knew from other HallowFests, although I wasn't completely sure what his trad was. Ragnar is about the size of a backhoe and wears his hair in two long braids. But we weren't the only ones there.

Most of the people there were carrying signs—signs that said things like "THERE IS ONLY 1 GOD" and "WITCHES BURN IN HELL." One of them carried a blow-up photo of Harm clutching a Bible and looking insincere, but then almost anyone looks shifty in studio portraits.

Mrs. Cooper was standing on the porch, trying to be

heard over the din. I put on speed and left Maidjene behind.

It's hard to reconstruct what happened next. At the time, everything seemed to happen at once, and all of it so loud and confused it was more bewildering than scary. And at the time I wasn't even sure who the demonstrators were; later I found out they were some of the more apocalyptic members of Harm's congregation, something I could have figured out for myself if I'd had the time.

Time. Everything comes down to time, in the end.

The demonstrator carrying Harm's picture climbed up on the porch. He had a megaphone in his other hand. Mrs. Cooper tried to push him off the porch. He started a long harangue through the megaphone; it merged with the rest of the noise. I heard various versions of it later; it was the usual sort of mudslinging about how we were evil and they were threatened, yadada, yadada, vamp till ready. The Pagans—and more were arriving every minute—began chanting "The Goddess Is Alive: Magic Is Afoot," drowning him out.

Then someone grabbed Iduna.

She's Ragnar's daughter and she's four—something I know only because she was born at a HallowFest when Sandy—her mother—went into labor two weeks early. She was wiccaned before she was a day old, with half the Pagan clergy of the Eastern seaboard in attendance. She didn't know what was going on, but she wanted her daddy, and went zipping toward him out of nowhere like a little blonde comet.

One of the demonstrators grabbed her in midflight and started going on about "rescuing the children." I got there just in time to grab Ragnar's arm as he went surging forward, and got banged in the jaw for my troubles.

A television van pulled up.

Maidjene made it to the porch. She isn't fast, but she's strong. She got the megaphone away from the godshouter. I don't know whether he fell or made a tactical retreat, but he ended up sitting at the foot of the porch steps.

"Let go," Ragnar said to me. He sounded in control, so I did. So did two other people. The van opened. Someone with a minicam got out, along with several people who didn't have minicams. Iduna was screaming. Ragnar pushed through the crowd, heading for her.

It sounds more orderly than it was—and quieter, and slower—but what it really was like was everything happening at once, and loud.

Ragnar plucked Iduna away from a man with glasses who was glad enough to let her go when he saw what was coming for her. Sandy ran up, screaming for her daughter. Ragnar handed Iduna to her. Then—in a calm, considered, in-control fashion—he punched the guy who'd grabbed Iduna bang in the face.

Everybody started yelling.

Mrs. Cooper—using the megaphone this time—started demanding that everyone get off her land. Nobody wanted to listen to her when they could talk to the local news crew. Maidjene went down and took the minicam away from the person using it. Ragnar helped her.

It was a mess.

I did my part for crowd control by making everyone who'd listen to me move back. Ironshadow showed up, having run all the way from the barn, and more people listened to him than to me. By now most of HallowFest had shown up to watch the raree show. I could see Mrs. Cooper down by the van, talking to the local television personality, with Maidjene hanging over her shoulder and some of the picketers trying to horn in. I wondered where Larry was; he'd love being ringmaster at a media circus.

While all this was going on, a black van drove up and found the television van blocking the road. The driver began leaning on the horn.

"It would really help if you guys would leave so those freaks didn't have an audience," I said for what seemed like the ten-thousandth time. Some took my advice. Some didn't.

A vision in black got out of the passenger seat of the van. She looked as if she'd come from an alternate universe where H. P. Lovecraft had done the costume design for *Annie Hall*.

Xharina.

Or to give the lady her full title, Xharina, Princess of Pain; the HPS and only woman member of a flourishing leather coven based in Brooklyn Heights. She was wearing black leather hotpants, artistically-ripped black tights screen-printed with skulls and roses, lace-up black paddock boots, a black lace merry widow, and a black velvet bolero jacket. The answer to an electronic journalist's prayer, although not to ours.

I couldn't hear well enough to make out what the representatives of the media were saying, but from the gestures, Xharina was inviting them to get their van out of the way. A sheriff's car pulled up behind Xharina's van, with all the lights on its lightbar flashing. I headed for Maidjene, hoping I wouldn't be followed. The film crew trotted over to the sheriff's deputy for a statement. The demonstrators waved their signs feebly.

"Need any help?" I said to Maidjene.

"Only if you can change time, speed up the harvest, or teleport me off this rock," she said, quoting *Star Wars* this time. "God damn them," she added, meaning, I supposed, the demonstrators.

The deputy was explaining that the demonstrators did not have the right to demonstrate on private property, but that they could walk up and down Route 6 all they wanted. The newscaster was trying to get the deputy to say that Harm had died in an "execution-style" killing. The demonstrators' spokesman was saying something about the heavy hand of divine judgment being made manifest, having apparently forgotten that it was Harm who'd died, not one of us. The guy Ragnar'd punched was nowhere in sight, for which small mercy I thanked the Goddess fervently.

"What the *fuck* is going on here?" Xharina demanded, New Yorker to the core.

"The local fundamentalist sphincter got hisself killed up here last night," Maidjene said. "Welcome to Hal-lowFest."

"Jesus H. Christ," Xharina said reverently. "For real?"

Why did people keep asking that?

"He isn't only merely dead; he's really and sincerely dead," I said. Two can play at Dueling Quotes. "Hi, Xhar."

"Hi, Bast. Um, look, do you guys think we could maybe get up to the barn? We've been driving since six this morning."

Maidjene looked at the traffic jam doubtfully. "Maybe," she said dubiously.

I looked around. Were there fewer of Harm's congregation gathered 'round than there had been a few minutes ago? I watched as another one plodded down the road in the direction of his parked car. Yup. Apparently none of them was in the market for the martyr's crown today.

After that, things broke up in stages.

The TV people headed back to their van. Xharina ran back to hers. The sheriff's car backed out of the way, lights still flashing, and it and the other two vans did some fancy backing and filling before they got themselves sorted out. The two vans went in opposite directions. The patrol car pulled up in front of Mrs. Cooper's porch; it was driven by a deputy I hadn't seen before.

I didn't want to be here. Big-time.

"I gotta go talk to them," Maidjene muttered.

"I'll see you later," I said, and walked back up to the barn through a jumble of standing gawkers.

What was I running away from? It seemed like I hadn't done anything since I'd gotten here except try to be someplace else from where I was, and I was getting tired of the lifestyle.

There were some easy explanations. I'd more or less broken with Changing, which meant it was time to form a coven of my own, something I'd so far avoided. Belle would expect it. *I* expected it, come to that. But it was a step I'd hesitated over taking for years, for reasons that probably weren't very good.

And then there was Julian and last night. He wasn't the type for one-night stands. Why him? Why me? Why now? And what next? Did we have more of a relationship than having worked together on *La Tesoraria del Oro* could give us? Was this love? Infatuation? A death wish? Whatever it was, it was going to have to take care of itself for a while longer; I had too much else to do. But I was still tired of running away from it.

Xharina's people were unloading their van when I got back up by the cabins. I saw Cain, Lasher, and Arioch, all of whom I'd met before, and two others I hadn't. I wandered over.

"Welcome to HallowFest," I said in my most orotund voice.

Xharina laughed. "Come to the country; it's quiet and safe. Yeah, sure. Where should we check in?"

I was abruptly reminded that I was carrying a parkaful of burglary equipment to make a gypsy switch on the registration forms. "Um, well, they aren't checking registrations any too closely now, so why don't you just come and get your badges?"

"Sure. You haven't met Goth and Riff-raff, have you? Guys, this is Bast."

Goth and Riff-raff, like their brethren, were dressed in the fashion of Biker Sluts from Hell: lots of denim and leather and visible tattoos, a look to which I am unreasonably partial. Goth had a glorious handlebar mustache and ferocious white sidewalls; Riff-raff was skinny and blond. Goth held out a paw in a fingerless leather glove. We shook. I could feel calluses scrape my fingers, and when I looked down I could see stars and letters inked into his fingers, blurry and dark.

Jailhouse tats.

It didn't make me suddenly decide Goth had killed Harm. But it did make me think about the fact that many of us come to the Community with a history of violence elsewhere. We've forged new family ties after so much loss and pain that we would defend these new families unthinkingly if the moment came. I remembered the psychic charge that had flashed through the crowd when one of the demonstrators had grabbed Iduna. Had Harm threatened one of us last night?

"Mars to Bast," Xharina said.

"Oh, yeah, right. Come on, I'll show you where you can put your stuff."

The room where Deputy Twochuck had been interviewing people was still empty, for a wonder, and had bunks for six. Renny and his ink pad were long gone; I showed Xharina and Goth in to it. Goth dropped the duffel bag he'd been carrying in a corner. It clanked.

"You can crash here; kitchen's around the corner if you want to cook, but it's going to be mobbed," I said dubiously. It's a regular apartment-style kitchen; the fact that almost a hundred people get fed three meals a day out of it each HallowFest weekend is one of Life's little miracles.

"Where are we playing?" Xharina said.

I remembered that I'd seen "Hoodoo Lunchbox Unplugged" on the schedule for tonight.

"If it doesn't rain, probably up at the Bardic Circle, after the Opening Ritual. I think—" I closed my eyes for a moment to concentrate on what I'd seen on the program when I'd skimmed it earlier. "Right. Lorne's scheduling the performers, so you'd probably better talk to him."

"We're going on first," Xharina said. I wasn't the one to argue with her.

"I'll help you unload."

It's amazing how much gear even an unplugged band travels with. Guitars, drums, flutes—all in cases—plus the usual bags, baggage, and unattached leather jackets. Not to mention the giant Coleman ice chest full of beer. I helped them stow everything and copped a brewski for my trouble, which I needed by then. Officially HallowFest is a "dry" site; in practice, this means a "don't ask, don't tell" policy on the part of Mrs. Cooper, and keep the bottles out of sight.

Xharina looked at my copy of the program doubtfully. It was a little after two, and according to the schedule we were missing "Fundamentals of Good Ritual," "Raising Pagan Children," and "Worshipping Aphrodite Safely." Maidjene had been ambitious—there was multitrack programming for most of the weekend.

"Um, we aren't really into most of this," Xharina said, looking from the program to me.

"Think of it as a networking opportunity. Some people go to them, some don't. And there's always the shopping."

"Oh, right, I heard Ironshadow was going to be here," Xharina said, picking up my allusion without a dropped beat. I wondered where she knew him from; she didn't look like the SCA type.

"Where's Bast?" I heard from outside the room, and, with a parting wave to Xharina, I went to see who wanted me.

It was Maidjene. And despite all probabilities, she asked me to cover Registration from three to five after all.

Half an hour later, I slithered into the registration cabin and shut the door—reasonable enough, as it was chilly outside. The box was still right where it had been when Sabine pointed it out to me.

I wondered what the Sheriff's Department was doing just now. I wondered if Harm'd had any next of kin to notify. I wondered who the "everyone" that Fayrene'd said hated him was. I wondered if I could find out.

And I wondered how it had happened that Harm had lain down and let someone—never mind who—pull open his clothes and stab him through the heart with whatever he'd been stabbed through the heart with. It occurred to me that Ironshadow would be a pretty good man to ask about edged weapons that made a Y-shaped entry wound. I made a mental note.

I knew what I intended to do here, and there was no point in putting it off. The doors of the cabins can be locked from the inside, and I pushed the lock button in on the knob. And that single act of commission opened the door for all the rest.

I didn't have to mean to give the forms to the Sheriff's Office, I told myself mendaciously. Just to keep Maidjene from burning them. In case she changed her mind.

But she wasn't going to change her mind. I knew that.

I slid the ribbons off the box. It was sealed with only a couple of licks of tape, and I sliced right through them with the box-knife. The registration forms were inside.

If Maidjene did change her mind before tonight and opened the box—or found out what I'd done in some other way—I would lose her friendship. Guaranteed. If she never found out, all the rest of the years of our friendship would be built on a lie.

What was important enough for me to betray a friend for? A dead man I'd despised?

Yes. Exactly that. Because Jackson Harm had been murdered. And if we do not count murder to be so extraordinary a crime that we will take extraordinary measures to punish it, we devalue human life, and with it, all hope of human dignity.

It was cold in my ivory tower, but I didn't mind it so much now. Because if the Goddess came to me and set a price that *I* would have to pay for justice, I knew now that I was willing to meet that price.

It is such folly to be wise.

I took the registration forms out of the box and put them in my jacket pocket and put the Tree of Wisdom catalogues into the box and sealed it back up just the way it had been. The ribbons would cover the cuts in the tape, if anyone bothered to look that closely.

I was easing the ribbons back into place when someone rattled the knob and then started banging on the cabin door. I froze like any burglar, clutching the violated box with both hands. Despite my lofty moralizing, I wasn't exactly eager to be caught.

"Bast?" A man's voice, elusively familiar. "Maidjene said you were in here! I've been looking for you all morning." The knob rattled again. "Open the door."

It was Lark.

5

I hadn't seen Lark in about ten years—he'd been the wild liberating fling I'd had in my twenties, when no one knew that sex could kill you and I'd been more willing to collect emotional scars than I became after I had a few. I don't know if we'd been in love with each other or just with ourselves—the mind edits memory, looking for the comfort level in history. Eventually, you even forget why leaving seemed to be such a good idea at the time.

I flung open the door and it was like stepping back through time. He'd aged, but not much. Not enough to count.

Lark has blue eyes and long brown hair. He looks like some kind of beardless hippie Jesus, and I've never seen him wear much that wasn't denim. That hadn't changed. He had on jeans and engineer boots and a chambray shirt with a denim jacket over it. He held his hair back with a rolled red bandanna tied as a headband. There was a gold ring in his ear.

"It *is* you!" I said, which is what people say when the other person still looks the same. People had been telling me for months that Lark was heading back East, but seeing him still came as a surprise.

He hugged me but we didn't kiss—thus the nineties

make cowards of us all. Why hadn't I been a coward yesterday, when it could have done me some good?

"Yeah. You're looking good, girl—somebody told me this morning you'd got in last night, but every time I went looking for you, you weren't there."

"You were here?" I said.

"Since Thursday. I laid low until I saw Phil show up Friday and then I came down and said hello—god, she gets fatter ever time I see her," he added with no particular malice.

"If you were married to Larry, you might, too," I retorted, moved to defend Maidjene after what I'd just done to her.

"Hell if I would," Lark said. "I'd give that cocksucker a Smith & Wesson enema and really make his day. Is he up here? Maybe I ought to go say hello?" Lark grinned at me.

"Oh no you don't." I dragged him inside. He flopped down on the villainous plastic couch in the boneless unselfconsciousness that old lovers have with each other.

"So what are you doing here? How long are you staying?" I asked. *Did you come to see me?* It would be nice to think so.

"Oh, well, looking up old girlfriends and generally hanging out," Lark said, waving a hand. "Just got back from a beer run; want one?"

I did, and he went out to his bike, parked outside. It was a top-of-the-line Harley, all gleaming maroon lacquer and streamlined farings: 25,000 dollars on the hoof; the price of a car. Lark lifted a six-pack out of one of the glistening steel saddlebags and came back inside. I used his absence to shove the ribbons all the way back into place on the box and dump it more or less where it had been. Crime accompli.

Then we sat there—with the door open, so Lark could watch his bike, which shouldn't be parked here anyway—

and talked about people we'd known and things we'd done. I'd had reports of him over the years; probably he'd had the same about me. And it was just about the way it had been, except for the fact that we were both ten years older and everything in the world had changed.

"So I hear you've quit Changing?" Lark said, popping the top on a second beer.

Maidjene would have told him that; it wasn't exactly a secret, Community gossip being what it was. "Sort of," I said cautiously, not wanting to go into all the gory details. This was my second beer in half an hour, and on top of a night of very little sleep, I could feel it hit me hard. Alcohol makes me reckless, which is good in a few situations. A very few. Not this one. Covens are like families; leaving is a combination of divorce and graduation. The impulse, after separation, is to justify your position.

"About time," Lark said, and changed the subject before it could get awkward. The conversation wandered on easily with no particular direction, until Lark remembered someplace else he had to be, and left to be there.

Once he was gone, I stared at the door and brooded—about something other than the state of my morals, for a change.

My breakup with Changing had been coming for years; Belle's style and mine had drifted too far apart, and enough had changed so that I was no longer willing to submit to her authority instead of to my intuition. The difference of opinion was irreconcilable and basic: Belle believed that magic was subjective and the Gods were allegories; that evil was a failure of social services and malice was a failure of perception.

It's a popular and comfortable viewpoint, which may be the reason I don't embrace it. Unlike Belle, I believed in the Goddess, Death, and Hell; in both true capital-E Evil and the lazy cowardice that often passes for it in the modern world; and also in a judgment that didn't wait conveniently on the sidelines until your next life.

And I wonder why I don't have more friends. But I didn't need more friends just now. I needed a coven, and the only way to get one was probably going to be to run one.

Lark had been Wiccan the last I'd heard, and probably still was if he'd come to HallowFest. He might be looking for an agreeable coven to join—or even to lead. It would be logical for us to pair off—I could hear the wheels turning in Belle's head from here.

But I didn't want Lark for my High Priest and working partner, I told myself, even if he was one hundred times more plausible material for the job than Julian would ever be (being, to begin with, a member of the same religion). Because Lark hadn't changed. I'd thought that the moment I saw him, and it was true, and seeing him again had reminded me freshly of all the reasons we'd split up.

He was charming. Yes, and thoughtless as well. He was compassionate. And had a violent temper. He was faithful—in his fashion. He was good in bed. And believed in that old double standard: men stray, women pray.

In short, Lark was the sort of person you probably couldn't stand unless you were in love with him.

And I wasn't. But there was enough friendship there to make part of me want to work to tip us back over the line into love—you can do that, if you work at it—and that would be a stupid thing to do, although it would probably feel very good for quite a while. And feeling good would be nice. For a change.

I didn't realize until I'd framed the thought that the emotional disquiet that had been vaguely dogging me all day came from the fact that my little tryst with Julian hadn't left me feeling good, answer to my girlish fantasies though it had been. Oh, not that it had been any species of rape, even by the PC rubber yardstick in use these days, but it had left me feeling unsettled, uncertain of my ground. A nice normal dysfunctional relationship with Lark would at least be something I could understand. That was the thought that led to me wondering how Lark and Julian would react to each other when they met, and the despairing certainty that they would meet, and I would probably have worked myself all the way up to quiet desperation if Glitter hadn't stuck her head in the cabin door.

Glitter is one of my (former) coven-mates in Changing, and a friend (still). In real life, Glitter is a probation officer for the City of New York, a gritty reality she offsets as much as possible by the way she dresses. To call Glitter's clothing "eccentric" is to be far too conservative—I honestly don't know where she comes up with some of her outfits, but clothes aren't clothes to Glitter unless they are purple or sparkly or, preferably, both.

Which meant that for a nature festival at a rural campground, Glitter had chosen to manifest in a deep violet sweatshirt and sweatpants combo liberally decorated with gold and fuchsia fabric paint, sequined rickrack, and the odd rhinestone. She was wearing an outdated down jacket made of metallic purple rip-stop nylon, which, fortunately, coordinated with the other pieces. To see Glitter and Maidjene together is to be aware of what a pallid, colorless world we normally live in.

"Oh, hi," Glitter said. "You're still here."

"Uh-huh," I said. "And if I'm still here in half an hour, I'm going to stick you with it—I'll have to close down the Snake's table for the night." And see Julian again.

"Oh, well, Lark said you were here," Glitter said. She sounded nervous for some reason. It couldn't be the murder, considering what Glitter does for a living, although it's different when it happens on your own time.

"He was right," I said. "Here I am. How are you?"

"Are you going to work with him?" Glitter burst out breathlessly.

In Paganspeak that phrase has only one interpretation: Glitter was asking me what I'd been asking myself: if I intended to take Lark for my working partner if—
when—I founded my own coven. That I would have to find someone—and a male someone at that—was something neither of us questioned; it's a basic tenet of the particular branch of ritual magic from which Gardnerian Wicca is descended. Each coven has a High Priest and a High Priestess, male and female to mirror the God-and-Goddess duality that we of the Wicca worship.

"I don't know yet," I said slowly, although a moment ago I'd thought I had.

"Well," said Glitter, a little wistfully, "I thought if maybe the two of you were going to start another coven, I'd like to go in with you."

That was a facer, as they said in the nineteenth century, and I finally gave the logistics of starting my own coven serious brain room. Covens split all the time—I'd separated from Changing—but if I hived off formally, I'd be entitled to ask if any of Changing's current membership wanted to join my new coven. I wondered who'd accept that offer. Not Topper and Coral; they're headed for a coven of their own as soon as they're ready. But Glitter'd just said she wanted in, and maybe Actaeon, which would be good; men are scarce in the Craft.

"I thought you liked working with Belle," I said aloud.

"I do!" Glitter said quickly. "But, you know, she's talking about retiring . . ."

"She is?" I said blankly. It was true I hadn't been to a meeting of Changing in almost four months, but I still would have thought someone would have mentioned *something.*

"Not formally, exactly. But you know, fifteen years is a long time—"

And in the Community, where five years is a lifetime, Belle's decade and a half of activity made her one of the Great Old Ones of our religion.

"I couldn't have a coven meet at my apartment," I said, leapfrogging several intermediate questions.

"She wouldn't mind if we still met there," Glitter said.

It was true. In fact, as I knew, she'd revel in it: Belle has been feuding with her landlord, who has been trying to take the building co-op, for years. He considers every visitor she has a potential illegal sublet barring him from reclaiming what is wrongfully his.

But Belle quitting? This was a different kettle of fish: if Belle was thinking of retiring from coven leadership, she was either thinking of passing the coven to someone else or freezing its current membership and finding new places for all its members before she stepped down.

I didn't want Changing—it was a basic disagreement with Changing's "corporate culture" that had led to my leaving. I could see Topper and Coral taking over the magical entity that Changing had become without any problem, although if they did, Changing would move with them to Co-op City.

But a new coven . . . Meeting at Belle's but not belonging to Belle. Something different. Something new.

Suddenly it began to seem possible.

"I'll talk to Belle," I said.

Glitter grinned. I felt a heart-clutching pang of responsibility. But I was getting used to it.

So I thought.

Sabine showed up a few minutes later—mostly to tell me I didn't have to hang out here anymore.

"Anybody needs any registering they can come find us

over at the barn," she said. "Everybody's probably already here, anyway," she added. By Saturday at 5:00 they'd better be.

"Okay," I said. "You need any more help, just ask."

Glitter and I headed for the barn. The registration forms were heavy in the pocket of my parka. I steeled myself not to look back at the box.

I found that, in my absence, the rest of the HallowFest merchants had arrived and set up, including another bookseller and someone from the Witches and Pagans Outreach Network (WAPON). We were about eight tables all told, including Ironshadow's and the Snake's. Hallie's tie-dye robes were hung along a cord suspended between two nails driven into the low ceiling beams. At the other tables were a candlemaker, someone with oils and incenses, and a bakery sale table covered with things that looked better than any alternatives I had available for tomorrow's breakfast—or tonight's dinner, come to that.

Julian was sitting behind the Snake's table, reading the expensive copy of *La Tesoraria del Oro.*

"You're going to ruin your eyes, reading in the dark like that," I said. The surface of the table looked as if it had been rearranged. I hoped sales had been good.

"You sound like my mother," Julian said, setting the book aside. It wasn't one of our *Tesoraria*s, I realized when I got a closer look: its leather binding gleamed with use and handling and the pages were no longer mashed flat in the way of book pages that have just come from the bindery. Julian's own copy, then. I wondered if he intended to do the *Tesoraria* Work.

He stood up. "What now?"

It took me a moment to remember that this was Julian's first HallowFest, just as it was for Xharina and the Klingons.

"Merchanting's over for the day. We pack up, then

there's dinner. Ritual starts at eight o'clock, Pagan Standard Time. After that's Bardic Circle."

Julian removed his glasses and began pushing them on his coattail. It made him look younger. Maybe more accessible.

"I don't want to go to the ritual," he said neutrally.

"That's okay," I reassured him. Some people don't. I'd be there, because the Opening Ritual at HallowFest is one of my personal touchstones.

"Fine, then," Julian said, as if we'd settled something. There was a pause. "I'm going to be doing a working tonight. I'd like to use the cabin."

It took a beat, but I translated that without effort: Julian wanted privacy. I'd like to think he felt as awkward and off balance as I did about what we'd done, and given time, I might be able to convince myself he did.

"Yeah, sure; I can always sleep in the van." Which would be cold, but not much colder than the cabins, and I might end up sleeping somewhere else anyway. I wondered if there was room in Ironshadow's tent.

"Good," Julian said. "I'll let you close up, then." He tucked his copy of *La Tesoraria* under his arm and walked off. I paused a moment to get used to the sense of relief I felt at one more postponement of a confrontation with Julian. *If there's going to be a confrontation at all,* I emended scrupulously.

I walked around to the seller's side of the table and began to tuck things away. Out of the corner of my eye I registered that Glitter had come upstairs. She stopped first at the bake sale table and then drifted over to me.

"Want one?" Glitter said. She held out a muffin. "Banana–chocolate chip. Oooh, what's that?" she said, peering down at the table.

I took the muffin. "The same stuff you can see any day of the week in New York," I told her, biting into the muffin. It was a little sweet for my taste, but I ate it anyway.

Glitter was admiring a pair of sugalite "point" earrings. Sugalite is purple, which makes it a natural for Glitter, though not naturally pointed—or for that matter, crystalline. The Snake stocks a wide variety of carved pseudo-crystal "points." (My favorite is turquoise, as turquoise in its natural state appears in masses resembling cottage cheese, but thanks to the mercantile magic of New Age Crystal Power, even turquoise is vended as a six-sided point-ended cylinder complete with a specious set of mystic "properties.")

"I'll take them," Glitter said, fishing her wallet out of her purple rip-stop nylon fanny-pack.

I took her fifteen dollars—a mere three times what the things had cost wholesale—and added the money and the sales slip to the cashbox. Someone from Summerisle came through, ringing a handbell to close Merchanting.

Glitter told me I was welcome to join Changing for dinner. I told her I'd be there. Then she went her way, and I was left to my own devices.

I picked up the nearest empty box and put both The Snake's *Tesorarias*, the jewelry, and a few other small, high-end items into it, then set the cashbox on top. The rest of the stock—mostly books, plus a few small plaques and statues—could take its chances with the reasonably honest HallowFest membership. I covered the table with a cloth. Beside me, Ironshadow was also closing up. He was taking all his inventory with him, though; his wares were more likely to take a walk than the Snake's were.

I set the box I was taking with me down on a flat space on my table and idled over.

"How's business?" I asked.

"You made up your mind about that knife yet?" Ironshadow said. He held it up. In the sunset light the copper sickle looked as if it had been dipped in blood. The opalized bone glittered faintly.

"What was that special order Julian picked up from

you today?" I asked. "I didn't see it out on our table."
Sometimes the Snake commissions pieces from Ironshadow, then retails them at an outrageous markup.

"Personal," Ironshadow said. "Silver blade."

He made a face. Ironshadow does not like to work in
metals that won't hold a cutting edge, even if most of his
work will never cut anything more substantial than air.
But he does do special orders, and some forms of ceremonial magic call for weapons of copper, silver, and even
gold.

"Well, I hope you soaked him for it," I said amiably, and
Ironshadow grinned.

"Some of us are having a private party after the Bardic
Circle. You're invited," he said.

"I'll be there." Ironshadow's parties involve home-
brewed mead. "And I'll take the *boline*." I'd figure out a
way to pay for it somehow.

He twirled it in his fingers and presented it to me butt
first.

"I can't pay you for it now," I said, alarmed.

"You'll pay when you can," he said. "I trust you."

The vote of confidence made me feel absurdly mellow.
I remembered the other business I had with Ironshadow.

"About Reverend Harm," I began.

Ironshadow grinned, showing large white teeth. "Yeah.
I'd been wondering myself where the hell somebody in
Gotham County came up with a *kukri*."

If you've seen Alec Baldwin's beautiful but stupid movie
version of *The Shadow*, you've seen a *kukri*: it's a Tibetan
ceremonial knife with the sort of three-flanged blade
that—if you stuck someone with it—would probably leave
the sort of hole that had been left in Jackson Harm. In
real life, of course, it doesn't fly around by itself, so someone had to have been holding onto it to make it do what
it did.

What was unlikely about this scenario is that the *kukri* isn't really so much a knife as it is a knife *symbol* used in Tibetan Buddhism. It's cast, not forged; the only ones I've seen are dull as a letter opener, if not duller.

And, like Ironshadow, I couldn't imagine where anyone would get one around here.

I took the Snake's box of goodies down to the van, and took the opportunity to transfer Maidjene's registration forms from my pocket to a better hiding place in the back of the van. I still didn't feel good about what I'd done, but the hell of it was, I would have felt equally bad about any of the other choices I could see to make, some of which involved Maidjene's being arrested. I would have liked it if there had been someone else around to tell me what to do, but Witches don't even allow that privilege to the Goddess.

Speaking of Maidjene, Larry's Warwagon was at the other end of the parking area. I could see lights on inside, although the shades were down: Larry Wagner, doing his Charles-Bronson-in–*Death Wish* vigilante imitation and draining his RV's batteries. I wished I believed he'd stay where he was and spend the rest of the night communing with his technology, but I couldn't manage that.

I locked the Snake's van, then went back up to the cabin; if I was going to be shut out tonight I wanted my sleeping bag and toothbrush.

The cabin was empty when I got there, although Julian'd been back to it; the *Tesoraria* I'd seen him reading upstairs in the barn was on the tray-table altar next to the mirror, and next to it was a newspaper-wrapped bundle that was probably his new Ironshadow knife. I grabbed my sleeping bag and pillow and tried to decide how much else I could carry in the one trip I was willing to make. I dumped the bedding by the door while I made up my mind.

Julian'd said he was going to do a working—what Pagans would call a ritual—tonight, and I saw no reason to doubt it. Lots of people took the opportunity presented by HallowFest to do some pretty intensive ritual. But Julian wasn't a Pagan; he was a Ceremonial Magician. What could *he* be working on, this far from all the special paraphernalia that magicians used?

The *Tesoraria*? I glanced guiltily at the door, then went over and unwrapped Julian's Ironshadow bundle. I saw the white gleam of fine silver—pure silver, not sterling, expensive as gold and just as soft—and the coarse, mock-ivory sheen of bone. This was out of *La Tesoraria*, all right. I knew the book reasonably well—although I'd only worked on it, not read it—the knife was part of the Adept's new tools, for use when *La Tesoraria*'s year of ritual preparations were complete. I wondered if it were really built to spec, and if so, where Ironshadow'd gotten a lamb's thighbone.

I wrapped the knife back up again, wondering why the sight of it made me so uneasy. The only thing a blade like that would ever cut or be able to cut was air.

"These our actors, As I foretold you, were all spirits, and Are melted into air, into thin air . . ." (*Tempest,* Act 4, Scene 1).

Suddenly I didn't care about my toothbrush and I didn't care about my clothes. I grabbed my sleeping bag and my pillow and fled as if there were someone there to chase me.

By the time I got back down to the van again the feeling was gone, and the aftermath of the adrenaline rush made me conscious of how tired I was. I glanced at my watch. Five-twenty. Four hours, at least, until the start of the evening ritual—assuming anything like an on-time start was being charitable. I opened the back doors of the van and climbed in, shutting them after me.

It was dark inside the van, and so cold that there was no particular smell to it, though I knew when it was warm the van ponged of all the oils and incense that had been spilled there over time. I spread out the dirty packing quilts to form a comfortable foundation, zipped my sleeping bag up into a bag again, and pulled off my boots and parka. Then I wriggled down into the bag, pulling my pillow in after me. HallowFest parties have a way of going on all night and I'd already been up for twelve hours at least on top of a short night; I was weary to the bone and thought I could best spend my time grabbing a catnap while the grabbing was good.

Once I was lying there, though, I felt false. Theatrical; as if I were not here to sleep, but, rather, to be *seen* to be sleeping for some unknown watcher who must be persuaded of the fact. I closed my eyes and tried to ignore the sensation, but it wouldn't go away, even when I actually did slide over the borderland into sleep.

Lucid dreaming is the flavor of the month on the New Aquarian Frontier; insusceptible to objective proof, like so much in our lives, because it relies on the subjective testimony of the participant. Put as simply as possible, to dream lucidly is to be aware that you are asleep and dreaming while you are doing so, and even to manipulate dream-events with the conscious mind. All of us do at least the former at some point in our sleeping lives. I prefer not to meddle, but to leave my dreams alone, searching for what they're trying to say through the mute symbol-driven interface dividing the conscious and unconscious mind.

And so I let myself be carried from reverie into dream, without really noticing the moment when I crossed over.

It seemed logical to me to be back up in the pine forest, since I'd spent so much of the day there, at least in spirit. I wanted to talk to Jackson Harm: I wanted him to tell me what he was doing here at this hour of the morning.

Associative memory happily presented me with the leopard frozen in the snows of Kilimanjaro. No one knew why it had been there, either.

In my dream I realized that there was an appointment I must keep; a rendezvous that I was unaware of, although I'd begun planning for it years ago. The night was both Friday night and Saturday night—Jackson Harm was somewhere in the woods—alive—at the same time the Saturday bonfire blazed in the meadow below. The irrational conflation of images common to dreams made perfect sense, too, although they did cause me to suspect I was asleep. The bonfire shed no light here where I was, and there was something waiting for me in the wood.

Half-aware, I dismissed this thought as a shopworn Jungian archetype: the wood is a symbol of the preverbal unconscious, and there's *always* something waiting in it for the unwary traveler. But at the same time I knew that this wood was objectively real on some level, and so was what waited—a particular something, and no archetype—and whatever it was, to see it truly would change me forever.

To be changed like that frightened me even while I disbelieved in it: with my waking mind, I knew that the only thing that could be in this wood was the dead body of Reverend Harm, which I'd already seen. The dead body whose sight had changed me was in the past: Miriam Seabrook, whose murder I'd avenged, if not exactly solved. These woods are dark and dangerous, I'd told her once, but it had been too late to save her even then.

And when I remembered that, suddenly Miriam was here, clutching at me and demanding that I *see* before it was too late.

Now I realized these were dreams, not thoughts. I wrenched myself free and found I was standing at the edge of the fire pit, certain now that I was awake and pseudo-remembering that I had fallen asleep at the Bardic Circle. It was dawn, and I was thinking "what a strange dream *that* was" when I saw that what I'd thought were the campfire's remains were charred bones, burnt but recognizable—

And then I did wake up.

It was pitch-dark inside the van; I thrashed around disorientedly until I banged my face against the side and came completely awake, completely conscious of where I was. My heart was racing, and the dream images were already fading. The pine forest. Miriam. A dead fire of bones. A dream-pun that, I realized: bon-fire = bone-fire; an etymology that Murray, among others, cites in her work on premodern witchcraft.

I sat up, rubbing my eyes. The glowing numbers on my watch-dial told me it was a little after six pip emma, but I didn't feel like trying for sleep again if *that* was the sort of thing that was waiting for me in Dreamland. Dead friends and an urgent sense of mission: now *there's* hubris for you. Lady Bast, Lone Ranger of the Wicca, off on another quixotic quest for truth, justice, and the Aquarian Way.

Forget it. There were real live police investigating this homicide, and no place in their investigations for a talented amateur, or even me. Fayrene had told me what help I could be, and I'd been it, and that was that. I'd get in touch with her tomorrow, probably, and give her (maybe) the HallowFest registration forms I'd stolen, and that would be that.

And though I've made a career out of listening to what I didn't want to hear and seeing when it would be more comfortable to be blind, I told myself there would be enough time later to see what needed to be seen in the landscape of my dreams. And so I wormed out of the sleeping bag in the darkened van, wishing I'd had the brains to bring a flashlight down with me. Wishing I was warmer. Wishing.

*   *   *

There's a lot of distraction to be found at a HallowFest on a Saturday night if distraction suits your fancy. I'd seen lights on in the cabin I now only nominally shared with Julian. I hadn't stopped.

The dinner hour was just getting under way when I got back up to the barn around seven. It was warm in the barn—a combination of the now-functioning radiators and all the bodies packed into the area. People flowed into and out of the kitchen area in a random tidal fashion, sharing and offering food to anyone who passed; no one at the Festival would go hungry tonight. I mingled, searching out old friends and new acquaintances.

The Klingons had brought "Romulan ale"; whatever it was, it was luridly blue and wonderfully alcoholic. They'd also brought a whole Boar's Head deli roast beef, which they were eating in chunks off their daggers, which drew a few looks even from people who did the same thing themselves at SCA events. I introduced Orm Klash to Belle.

Belle was cool—she invited Klash's tribe to join Changing's meal and started trying to sell him on the idea of attending one of her monthly Pagan Leadership meetings. The fact that he was dressed out of a TV show and speaking every other sentence in interstellar Esperanto was something she appeared not to notice, but then, Belle was a red diaper baby and believes in Solidarity *Uber Alles,* which is part of the particular rock and hard place that's led to our (amicable) parting of the ways. I moved on, and found Lark partying with Hoodoo Lunchbox, as was (surprise) Actaeon. I joined them, and Ironshadow joined us, and everything was all right.

For a while.

". . . all I can say is, it'd be nice if somebody persecuted them for a change," Lark was saying after two or three beers. "Hell, what's wrong with one fewer Christo-Nazi in the world? Fire up the barbecue, boys, and throw another Christian baby on the coals, right?"

"*They'd* kill *us,* if they had the chance," a boy in this year's HallowFest T-shirt said solemnly. I wondered if I'd ever been that young.

" 'Never again the burning.' " Someone on the group's outskirts quoted the old radical tag line. It's a highly romantic concept: claim some suitably persecuted ancestors and write yourself a moral blank check for anything you choose to do.

"That is a stupid and evil idea," I heard myself say loudly.

"Well, who the hell are you?" T-shirt said.

Who do I have to be? as James T. Kirk is fond of saying. "Do you really think that anybody has the right to kill somebody else just because they worship a different god?" I said.

"Christians do," T-shirt said smugly, as if that were either entirely true or an answer.

"Look, he didn't mean anything," a woman next to T-shirt said. "You're overreacting."

"If he didn't mean anything he should shut the fuck up," I said, getting to my feet. "I'm sick of hearing people cheer on a murderer in order to pretend they're sanctimonious little right-thinking Pagans—especially you," I said to Lark. I felt my hackles rise: anger and power are closely linked; it's one of the tragedies of the Left-Hand Path. I headed out the front door before I either started crying or said something worse.

Before I made it outside I heard jumbled scraps of talk behind me: "Who does she think *she* is?" "Jonathan, you dickface." "She's the one that found Jesus Jackson." "Asshole." "I didn't *mean* anything."

Belle and Ironshadow were the ones who came out after me—not Lark. Ironshadow must have gone to get her. They put their arms around me to let me cry, but I couldn't. All I could do was quiver with trapped emotion and wish there was some barricade to clamber up onto.

"It isn't right they should be glad he's dead," I finally managed to say. It wasn't what I meant; that was too lofty a moral high ground for even me to defend.

"They're just assholes," Ironshadow rumbled soothingly.

We were standing just outside the "front door" of the barn, the main entrance that nobody uses during a HallowFest because all the action's in the other direction. There was enough light spilling through the uncurtained windows for me to see Belle and Ironshadow's faces, and to see a worried clump of people silhouetted in the open doorway. People who cared about me—or cared about something at least. Maybe just their own self-image.

"I understand how you feel, Bast," Belle said. "It must have been very scary to be the one to find the body. Sometimes when something like that happens people feel responsible for the fact that it happened, and then, because they can't do anything about it, they get angry. But you're not responsible. Reverend Harm's death isn't anything to do with you."

"No man is an island . . . any man's death diminishes me . . ." Do not ask for whom the John Donne's, it tolls for thee. I shook my head, choking on the words I both wanted and didn't want to say. "You didn't see him," I finally managed, which wasn't what I meant, either.

"It's over," Belle said firmly. "We have to bless it and let it go."

"It isn't real to them," Ironshadow said. "You know that. It's just another TV show. That's why they're talking like that."

"Cowboys and Indians," I said, drawing a deep, hurting breath. Pagans and Inquisitors. Choose sides, and let the dead not be real people, but merely a convenient way of keeping score.

"That's right," Belle said, giving my back an encouraging pat. "You're upset, that's all. Nobody really wanted Reverend Harm dead."

"Someone did, Belle," I pointed out. I stepped back, breathing deeply to center myself.

"That is nothing to do with you," Belle said firmly. But it was, even if only to the extent that I had to hold an opinion about the morality of the death I'd discovered.

"All right," I said. Belle took it as an agreement, but it wasn't. Not really.

They took me back inside; I got a lot of soothing mothering, and Lark even showed up and apologized, although neither of us was certain quite for what. He put his arm around me and I leaned back against him, both of us pretending it was ten years ago and none of the time between had happened.

And then it was time for the Closing Ritual.

The Closing (Opening) Ritual doesn't begin HallowFest in any practical sense, since it's scheduled to take place at a time when the majority of the attendees have arrived. It's the one event at which most of the Festival's attendees can usually be found—though not, as I've said, all. The parents of the very young often stay away (although children are welcome), as do those who don't fancy a long walk in the dark for reasons of health or hedonism. This year more people than usual elected to stay behind in the barn, at least as far as I could tell from my place in the procession.

The ritual begins with the Closing Ritual that goes with the Opening Ritual of the previous year's HallowFest; closing the Festival just before opening it again (bad magical discipline though it is) is a conceit that helps us take the love and belonging we feel here with us through the secular year, as if in some sense we never leave this sacred ground.

Most people change into ritual gear for the opening, and I'd even brought my robe to the Festival, but it was in the cabin and I didn't want to disturb Julian at whatever his private devotion was to retrieve it. I had on the silver cuff bracelet that marks my degree in my particular Wiccan tradition and the pentacle I always wore and that was sufficient.

The flashlights people carried made brilliant erratic searchlights through the country night. It took maybe twenty minutes for all of us to reach the Bardic Circle, and members of Summerisle Coven were already there. They'd marked out the circle boundaries with battery-operated Coleman lanterns. The bonfire had been built sometime this afternoon and now stood ready, surrounded by carved and illuminated jack-o'-lanterns from the pumpkin-carving workshop I'd missed, flickering orange-gold with dancing candle flames. Even with fewer people than usual attending we made a large circle—possibly ninety people. Most of us knew what to expect from previous years. We waited.

Enough different trads come to HallowFest each year that it would be exclusionary for whoever was running it to use the ritual form of any specific tradition at this circle, so we don't. The organizers of the last year's Festival begin by closing last year's circle, then this year's organizers open this year's circle. Then one of our youngest Pagans lights the fire. In practice, this means he or she will throw a bit of burnt branch saved from last year's fire onto the waiting woodpile, then retreat to safety while an adult lights it. As theater it's simple, effective, and healing, which is, I suppose, one of the reasons it's evolved the way it has.

While the fire catches we go around the circle, making personal statements and introducing ourselves. Sometimes we make sacrifices to the flames—on the HallowFest bonfire one year I'd burned diaries and papers for

Miriam Seabrook. I could see the ribbon-tied box that I'd tampered with earlier sitting at Maidjene's feet, and felt a guilty surge of relief. She'd burn it, and with it all evidence of what I'd done.

Unless, of course, somebody told her afterward.

Between them, the Coleman lanterns and the jack-o'-lanterns cast enough light that the yellow Crime Scene ribbons were visible at the edge of the clearing, an unwelcome reminder of reality. I could see the soon-to-be-fire in the fire pit: a stack of logs and split kindling almost three feet high, with a tinder-filled core for easy lighting.

Bailey from Summerisle stood in for members of Brightstone Coven in Vermont, who'd run HallowFest last year and couldn't make it down this year. He read out a short closing statement from them and then stepped forward and tucked the rolled parchment in among the logs in the fire pit.

Then Maidjene opened this year's HallowFest, while Sabine played "Banish Misfortune," an old Irish folk tune, on her flute. It was probably only my guilty conscience that made me feel Maidjene placed undue stress in her opening speech on HallowFest being "at a time out of time and a place out of the world, a sanctuary where hate and ugliness cannot enter."

I wished it were true.

This year Iduna carried the stick salvaged from last year's fire; she was wearing a light-colored robe that already had charcoal smears on the front and clutching Ragnar's finger as he led her up to the woodpile. There was a moment of negotiation before she'd let go and drop the branch into the kindling, and everyone clapped and cheered when she did. Ragnar picked her up and carried her back to the perimeter as she hid her face against his neck.

On the sidelines, Ironshadow lit a torch. It was a real torch—wax-soaked rags wrapped around the end of a

stick, and he flourished it to make sure it caught before
he handed it to another of Maidjene's coveners — Lorne, I
thought. He was wearing a Summerisle tabard and looked
as young as Wyler Pascoe. I wondered if that meant I was
getting old, or merely jaded.

The people who'd brought drums or other rhythm instruments to the circle — and many had — began to strike
them in time, falling quickly into synch. Lorne matched
his step to the beat, holding the flaring torch high over
his head.

It is at moments like these that the world seems to become truly real — as if the world that all of us occupy daily
were truly, as so many theologians tell us, merely a veil
for some unknown, but more briliant and resonant, truth.
It is this sense of intense reality — what C. S. Lewis called
"joy" — that brings us all to our varied spiritual paths, and
its lack that drives us ever onward, seeking.

Had Harm found this joy in serving his narrow and ex-
clusionist God?

The question jerked me back inside my skin and made
me feel cold and uncomfortable — and joyless. Lorne
shoved the torch into a hole in the pyre, and as the kindling caught the wood was illuminated from within like
the Halloween pumpkins ringing the base of the fire pit.
The drums, rattles, and tambourines exploded into an ar-
rhythmic din, over which the sound of Rebel yells and wolf
howls rang back from the surrounding trees. But the joy
that others found, or seemed to find, here did me no
good — I was cut off from it, trapped in my secular skin
without the confidence in the Lady's presence that I'd
come here to evoke.

The ritual proceeded. We went around the circle, each of
us saying our piece, whether coven affiliation, geograph-
ical location, or witty tag line.

"I'm Brandy, and I'm from Summerisle."

"I'm Carol from Boston, and this is my first HallowFest." ("Welcome, Carol!" we all shouted back.)

"Treath and Dan, Endless Circle."

"Pain is Truth! And I'm Xharina."

"Ironshadow—and this sure isn't my first HallowFest."
(Laughter. "Welcome, Ironshadow!" we shouted anyway.)

And on around the circle. "I'm Bast," I said, when it
was my turn. "I'm from Manhattan." And nothing else.

By the time I spoke the fire was burning strongly.

"For those who have yet to find us—let their voices not
be silenced!"

A woman I didn't know stepped forward and threw the
tambourine she'd been playing onto the fire. The drum-
face of it had been elaborately painted, and knots of ribbons trailed from the frame. A collective gasp went up
from all of us as it charred to black and then caught fire,
and I thought again about Wyler Pascoe, who wanted to
see "the Witches."

There were other gifts to the fire—someone's thesis; a
photograph of a loved one who'd died since this time last
year; even a *papier-mâché* Barney the Dinosaur filled with
incense. It flared strobe-bright before becoming a thick
column of scented white smoke.

Maidjene threw her box into the fire without saying
anything; its impact sent up a shower of sparks.

The circle opened out away from the fire pit as the fire
got hotter. Lots of people had brought instruments up
with them; there was music going on, and singing; a jug
of apple cider was passing and so was a box of cookies;
everyone was settling into the familiar *ur*-ritual mind-
space of a HallowFest Opening Ritual.

Everyone but me. No matter how hard I tried to concentrate on the ritual, I kept looking up the hill as if I expected Hellfire Harm to come striding down it brandishing a flaming sword.

Which was why I saw them.

The flickering firelight made for tricky seeing; at first I put the movement among the trees down to that. But it wasn't. There were people in the woods, coming down through them. Toward us. They might even be from the Sheriff's Office; I didn't know. I did know that their being here meant something was wrong.

We were making too much noise for a shout to carry, and half a lifetime's habit kept me from breaking across the circle to warn Maidjene. I grabbed the person next to me and pointed up the hill before stepping back to run *deosil* outside the circle's perimeter. As I ran I saw that one of the men was carrying a rifle.

A mob of Pagans is no brighter than any other mob. If we'd stood our ground and kept our heads, everything might have been all right. But someone screamed and then everyone was screaming, yelling, running in all directions. I grabbed Maidjene to keep from being swept away with them.

"Call the police!" Maidjene yelled in my ear.

Assuming these *weren't* the police. I let go of her and ran blind, taking the shortcut down the hill, straight toward the lake. Behind me I heard a gunshot.

6

I slammed in one door of the barn.

"There's men with guns up at the circle! Call the police!" I ran out the other door, moving fast, blessing the Lady that through luck and miracle I wasn't wearing my ritual robe: black, wool-blend, and eight yards of material in the trailing skirt alone. I ran for Mrs. Cooper's house because I doubted the ability of any of the barn's inhabitants to get the sheriff's deputies here as fast as she could, but I was gasping and winded by the time I jumped her front porch steps and banged on the door.

"Police," I panted, as she opened the door.

She let me inside. She was already on the phone—to the Sheriff's Office, as a matter of fact.

"One of them's here now, Tod," she said into the receiver. She looked at me. "I heard shots."

I'd forgotten how far sound carried in the country—she'd probably heard us howling, too. "Men with guns," I gasped. "Crashing the circle. Through the pine forest." My throat felt as if it had been blow-dried.

"She says there are men up here with guns," Mrs. Cooper told the phone. There was a pause. "Tod Fulton, do I resemble an utter fool to your mind? Of course I'll stay here and let you take care of it. That's what you're paid for."

She hung up the phone and came back to me. I was standing, bent over and blowing like a grampus who's just finished running the New York Marathon.

"Are you all right?" she asked. Her voice was kind.

I nodded, still puffing. My heart was a hard palpable thudding in my chest and my mouth tasted of salt and iron. I hadn't run that far that fast in years, and adren-aline—like magic—takes its toll.

"Come sit down," Mrs. Cooper said. "You're . . . ?"

"Bast," I said. "I've got to—"

"You stay right here," Mrs. Cooper told me firmly. "No one needs you running around in the dark."

It was good advice. Come to that, I really didn't want to go. I have the greatest respect for the power of a gun in the hands of an agitated lunatic. I'd faced one once, and it'd be fine with me if I never did again. I came and sat at Mrs. Cooper's kitchen table. She gave me brandied coffee and shortbread biscuits.

As I was sitting there I saw a red/white/blue blaze flash by the windows, then a few seconds later heard a squib of siren as the car cleared the road ahead. The Gotham County Sheriff's Department had arrived.

"John'll take care of things," Mrs. Cooper said.

"They're going to love coming here twice in one day," I said.

Mrs. Cooper laughed harshly. "More than that—I had them up here Friday in the pee em to toss Mr. Hellfire Jackson Harm out on his ear. I don't know what anyone else may have to say about it, but for my money, Reverend Harm's decease is the best thing that could have hap-pened in all of Gotham County."

Loved everywhere he went, just as I'd thought. "Harm was up here Friday?" I asked.

Mrs. Cooper sat down opposite me at the kitchen table and sipped her own spiked coffee. "Hellfire was up here *every* year before you people were due in, saying I should throw you all out on your ears. I said to him Friday—just like I do every year—'Just you tell me, Jackson Harm, where I'm going to get another party—in October, mind— to rent the whole campground for three-four days'—well! Being practical was *not* any of Jackson Harm's particular virtues, let me tell you; he never did have an answer to that one. But this year he outdid himself."

I was burning to ask her how, but just then another police cruiser pulled up. This one stopped, and the doorbell rang.

"Just you look at this and see what I mean," Mrs. Cooper told me, getting out of her chair to answer it. She took a pamphlet out of a kitchen drawer and plunked it down in front of me, then went off to the door. "*That's* what Mr. Harm was doing up here Friday," she shot back over her shoulder.

I picked up the pamphlet. It was cheaply done: black and white, gatefold, probably just Xeroxed onto bond paper. It was typewritten, not typeset, and the columns ran crookedly up and down the page—a home paste-up job.

"Satan's Handmaids!" the front page said, in large blurry letters. Press-type probably, or lifted from something else. There was a hand-drawn Christian cross inside a barred circle beneath the words.

I skimmed it quickly, then read it more carefully as I realized that this wasn't just the standard sort of redneck godshouter rant, but one directed specifically at *us*.

"You say that all gods are one god, but there is only One God, who is the Christ Jesus, who has Truely [sic] said: Thou Shalt Have No Other Gods Before Me . . ."

If this was an example of Harm's theology, he was on pretty shaky ground: the speaker in that particular case wasn't the son, but the father, and it was one of the commandments given to the prophet Moses.

There was more. Our Goddess was no goddess, but the Scarlet Woman of Babylon (which, speaking from the purely anthropological viewpoint, which holds that the gods of the old religion become the devils of the new, was only true, but not in any way Harm would've liked); our souls would dwell in darkness because we preferred stones to the living bread of the Word; et cetera, et cetera, ad nauseam, *und so weiter.*

I could not imagine anyone at HallowFest being converted by this little tract: amused, yes, offended, possibly. It would offend most of the Christians of my acquaintance, come to that. The strangest thing about it was that apparently Harm meant this offensive little morsel of liberation theology to have a positive effect.

I folded the pamphlet back together. The back flap was an invitation—with map—for HallowFesters to join his Sunday Morning Rescue Prayer Service and be welcomed again into the whole body of Jesus Christ, a process which sounded mildly cannibalistic, to say the least.

While I'd been reading I'd been half-listening to what was going on in the background: Mrs. Cooper's voice interspersed with a male voice I didn't recognize. Now both of them came into the kitchen.

"I'm Sergeant Blake. You say you saw men with guns?" he asked me.

They grew them big in Gotham County—the sergeant was Fayrene's male counterpart, big and husky with the start of a spare tire around the middle, black hair instead of blond, and the addition of a large mustache. The gun was the same though: a Heckler & Koch .45 automatic with a ten-round clip. Businesslike.

"I saw a rifle," I said, not really sure now about *what*

I'd seen. "And about five men. And I heard a gunshot."

"Roy's radioed for an ambulance," Sergeant Blake said, which did not reassure me. "I'll be back to talk to you in a few minutes, so I'd appreciate it if you stuck around here for a while, ma'am."

Sergeant Blake left. I heard the cruiser drive off, and the blips and yelps of the siren that meant he was clearing the way ahead.

"Isn't that the stupidest piece of trash?" Mrs. Cooper said.

It took me a moment to refocus my mind from Sergeant Blake and his gun to the Reverend Harm's little essay.

"Well," I said inadequately.

"Wanted me to hand them out! Free! And I told him, 'Jackson Harm, as sure as I'm standing here those people are just going to laugh in your face! And why should I do your dirty work for you?'—well! Then he started rabbeting on about equal time, and I told him that this was a campground, not a presidential election, and then he said—bold as brass, *if* you please—"

It occurred to me that Mrs. Cooper was one of those speakers whose conversation doesn't require participants, merely an audience, and then I thought that she probably didn't get too much of either one. And so I would have listened even if she weren't telling me things I really wanted to hear more about. Certainly she'd had as many jarring shocks as I'd had that day, but where were the people for her to share them with?

Now that I'd had a chance to actually talk to Mrs. Cooper I could place her type: New England liberal, of the breed who will defend her fellow citizens' eccentricities to the death and demand the same tolerance for her own. A kind not much seen in these parts in recent years, more's the pity.

"*First* he tells me that *God* doesn't like the way I'm running Paradise Lake—well, I told him that *God* could tell me that in person, rather than sending a nasty little errand boy like him!"

I laughed at the joke, as I was meant to. It's amazing how many people who profess to believe in an omnipotent, omnibenevolent, omnidirectional, detail-oriented god still manage to believe that this god doesn't have either the time or the inclination to run his own errands.

"And if he thought that I didn't have God's home address, after having him in my Sunday Bible classes all those years—"

Harm, I supposed she meant, and not Harm's celestial supervisor. "And?" I prompted, finishing my coffee.

She got up to get the standing pot. Her hands were shaking, and I put it down to age, but when she turned around I could see it wasn't age—it was fury.

"He had the nerve—the absolute nerve, that jumped-up little brass-bound bastard—"

I blinked in surprise. Profanity is supposed to be the exclusive preserve of the young and trendy.

"—to tell me that if I let you people rent the place again this year, I could kiss good-bye to the Summer Youth Bible Study Camp!"

"The Bible Study Camp?" I echoed, trying not to look as baffled as I felt.

"*They* have Paradise Lake for July. *All* of July," Mrs. Cooper said.

Now it started to make sense, and as usual, the bottom line wasn't about theology, but money. A campground is like any other small business, and the margin between failure and survival is slight. One month of her peak season fully booked and occupied might very well make the difference between Paradise Lake's success and failure for Mrs. Cooper.

"Could he do that?" I asked.

She snorted and refilled our cups. "Just between you

and me and the gatepost, Jackson Harm wasn't quite the big stink he thought he was. But still . . ." Her voice trailed off. "Well, he won't be doing anything *now*, that's for sure!" she said in satisfied tones.

"And he was up here Friday?" I asked, just to be sure.

"Friday morning, bold as brass, preaching at me as if I were a public meeting for two and a half *hours*, until I had to call Tom down to the Sheriff's to disinvite him. And at that he left all of his damned pamphlets behind!" She jerked her chin and I saw three suspicious-looking boxes piled in the corner of the kitchen.

"And Saturday morning he was dead," I said.

"Up in my woods, which is pure meanness on his part. Have another cookie," Helen Cooper said.

So I did, while Mrs. Cooper regaled me with more local color from Jesus Jackson's glorious career. In addition to Mrs. Cooper, the Reverend Harm had harassed the local paper, the local radio station, and even the welfare office in Tamerlane, which is twenty miles up Route 6 and the closest thing to a city there is in Gotham County.

It occurred to me I'd just been handed a motive for murder that the Sheriff's Office would have no trouble understanding. Mrs. Cooper's.

She had motive—Harm was trying to drive away the customers on whom her livelihood depended: the Bible Camp and HallowFest. If she wanted to do a frame-up, she had enough experience from previous HallowFests to do a fair job of imitating our handiwork. And she'd had opportunity—by her own admission Harm'd been here Friday afternoon.

But so had Maidjene. And Lark. And probably even Larry Wagner in his Warwagon, all set to fight World War III and convinced that the world was against him.

No, I couldn't believe in Mrs. Cooper for the killer. If she were to kill someone—something I didn't doubt for a moment she was capable of—she wouldn't use a knife. A shotgun, maybe—I'd be surprised if she *didn't* have one. But Harm hadn't been shot. He'd been stabbed. And I didn't think Mrs. Cooper had the physical strength necessary to stab Harm, let alone the inclination to get him half-naked first.

The doorbell rang again. I glanced out the parlor window, but didn't see any flashing lights. Mrs. Cooper went to open the door.

"I just couldn't tear myself away," I heard Fayrene Pascoe drawl.

She came into the kitchen, still in uniform, this time with the addition of a dark green nylon bomber jacket.

"Hi, Fayrene," I said.

"You in trouble again?" she asked me amiably. The walkie-talkie on her hip chattered on intermittently, with flashes of static and 10-codes I wished I could interpret. I caught a burst of someone telling someone else to "secure the area," and hoped it meant the trouble was over.

"Some boys are up here bothering my campers!" Helen Cooper said fiercely.

"Jeff and Johnny are probably taking care of it, Mrs. Cooper; don't you worry. I heard over the radio one of your friends got shot, though—nothing serious," she added to me. "So I thought I'd come over and see the fun. What were you doing up there this time of night?"

"Trying to pursue that freedom of religious expression to which the Constitution theoretically entitles me," I said. I sounded as if I were spitting nails. "Sorry," I said after a moment. "It was our Saturday bonfire—"

"I've seen 'em. We had one of our units on a short drive-by tonight, but Tony didn't think we needed anybody out here," Fayrene said. After a moment I placed the name: Mad Anthony Wayne, our detective-on-the-spot.

"Well, we were all just standing there, and these guys started coming down from out of the pine forest, and one

of them had a gun—rifle or shotgun, I don't know—and I
ran like a rabbit," I said.

"More people should do that," Fayrene said.

When Fayrene walked me back up to the site it was glar-
ingly lit by the searchlights of two cruisers and looked
pretty well trampled. More cars not belonging to the festival were parked nearby, and I counted six uniformed
deputies, not to mention the EMTs and their big orange-
and-white truck, just now arriving. The deputies were
herding the HallowFesters into little clumps and chasing
after the ones who just wanted to leave. Babies were crying, and I looked automatically for Ragnar and Iduna. I
didn't see them, but I did see Xharina, standing next to
Klash and looking worried. There was an eerie continu-
ity between the two sets of leather, straps, buckles, and
elaborate makeup. I looked away before we could make
eye contact, following Fayrene.

There were flashlight beams as the deputies walked
the wood, blazing emergency lights, and blaring radios.
Fayrene sliced through the chaos as if it were familiar ter-
ritory, swapping jokes with the other deputies. In the
middle of it all, the bonfire Maidjene's coven had so
painstakingly constructed and lit blazed on, even with no
one there to care.

As is usual—though not, as I am starting to suspect
in my case, typical—I was on only the very fringes of the
whole thing and had to piece it together out of what I
found out later. Which was this:

It wasn't religious bigots so much as it was a case of
Saturday night and nowhere to go—and Paradise Lake
and its exotic visitors very much in the forefront of the
public mind, thanks to all the coverage in the paper and
on the local news about Harm's death.

When I passed one of the cars I was surprised to see
there was someone in the back—an older man, with the

undefinable air of being Not One of Us. He was wearing handcuffs and looked bored and irritated, which was better than I would have been doing in the same situation.

"So, John-boy, you managed to make any arrests yet?" Fayrene was addressing Sergeant Blake, whom I'd met earlier. "Oh, and I already took the statement of the original complainants."

Sergeant Blake looked at her, and then past her to me, then back again.

"Local boy," he said to her. "Nothing much. We can hold Arnold here on menacing—he had the shotgun. The worst we can charge his friends with is harassment, maybe a little conspiracy. They took Reece Wheeler off to Taconic Hospital—somebody plinked him with a .25 or a .32, and none of the boys here was carrying anything like that. So they say."

He looked back at me, while I figured the rest out for myself. Someone had been wounded tonight, but not someone from HallowFest. The victim had been one of the local party animals, one Reece Wheeler. And if Wheeler had been shot, and his fellow Jukes and Kallikaks disavowed it, the only other possible candidate for shooter was one of us—and no one was admitting to possessing the gun that had shot him.

"I didn't shoot him." I barely kept myself from saying I was glad he was shot and hoped it hurt. I was not prepared at all for the sheer triumphal fury that shook me at the thought that one of our attackers had been shot. At that moment, I wanted them all dead, as slowly and painfully as the hand of Man could contrive. I'd been terrified and I wanted revenge; it was a stupid, childish, clockwork reaction, and I tried very hard to regret it. "I don't know who shot him. I wasn't here." I had a witness to the last statement, at least.

"Any of your friends carry guns?" Sergeant Blake asked. "Anyone here we should talk to?"

"Not that I know of." And at that moment, I wouldn't tell him if I did. Fortunately the need to lie, if not the impulse, was absent.

Childish, like I said.

"Find it yet?" Fayrene asked.

Sergeant Blake made a spread-handed shrug that took in the entire scene, including the clumps of Pagans standing and watching. The entire area around the fire was littered with things people had dropped in the confusion: hats, wands, Pepsi cans, baby bottles—even an *athamé* or two.

"In *this*, Fay? We're going to sweep the woods in the morning, but sure as you're born that pop-gun's at the bottom of the lake by now. Nobody saw a thing, and Reece says he doesn't want to press charges, so you know how much rope the DA's going to give us."

"Well, that's mighty white of Brother Reece," Fayrene drawled, her flat upstate accent becoming more pronounced.

"Are you the officer in charge of this investigation?" It was Maidjene, sounding small and scared, but there. I raised my hand in greeting. Her eyes focused on me for an instant, then flicked away. Her face was whiter than it'd been this morning by Harm's body, an occasion that seemed a thousand years ago now.

Sergeant Blake turned to her. "I'm Sergeant Blake," he said.

"My name is Phyllis Wagner. I'm the organizer for this festival." Maidjene hesitated. "Can you stop them from coming back?"

"I don't think they'll try anything else, Ms. Wagner," Sergeant Blake said soothingly.

"You didn't think they'd try this, or you'd have left someone here to protect us," Maidjene said, shaky but dogged.

Blake looked at Fayrene, and some cryptic cop-thing seemed to pass between them.

"We'll have someone walk the area a few times tonight," Sergeant Blake told her. He didn't seem to know about the material Maidjene was supposed to turn over to his department, or maybe he was just being subtle. "Now, do you want to lodge a complaint?"

"I—" Maidjene hesitated, although I could tell she was mad and scared in just about equal portions. If she lodged a complaint there might be a trial where she'd have to testify, and that would be an awfully long commute for somebody who lived in Jersey and currently had no visible means of support.

"I'll complain," I said harshly. "I saw them coming down the hill. I saw the gun. I'll do it."

Maidjene's look of gratitude did little to salve my aching conscience.

"Are you sure about that, miss?" Sergeant Blake said, in that tone that suddenly makes you sure of nothing at all. I'd dealt with the law before, though, so I stood my ground.

"The fire was bright. He was close. The barrels reflected—on the rifle; even if they were blued, you could see them; they were metal. I knew he had a gun, and I knew he wasn't a member of HallowFest. We had trouble this afternoon. You probably saw it on the news. I thought this might be connected."

Blake asked for my name and address, and I gave them. I volunteered that I was selling here at HallowFest, and Maidjene told them that I was helping the committee running the festival, which was not really that far from the truth, all things considered.

"Did either of you see a shot fired? Anyone with a gun?" Sergeant Blake said, but not as if he expected to get the truth.

I shook my head. I'd been running down the hill when I heard shots.

Maidjene shrugged.

"Do you know anyone here who might have a gun?" Sergeant Blake went on. They must give out these lists of numbered questions in Famous Law Enforcement Officers Training School.

Maidjene and I got the same idea at the same moment, and stared at each other with identically transparent looks of horror.

"Larry," Maidjene said in a strangled voice. "Larry's got guns. Lots of them. He always takes them with him."

Not that I suspected Larry. The question was, had someone borrowed one?

The four of us went down to Larry's trailer. Along the way Maidjene filled them in: soon-to-be-ex-husband, survivalist, possessor of various firearms, and free-range pain in the ass. Neither of us had seen him up at the Circle, but that wasn't much in the line of an alibi.

I didn't think any more of it than that it was another episode in that embarrassing real-world sitcom: "The New Adventures of Larry," but as we got closer, it occurred to me that Fayrene and Sergeant Blake didn't share my insouciance about the upcoming interview. They stopped Maidjene and me at the edge of the parking lot and told us to stay here.

"Which one is it?" Sergeant Blake asked.

Maidjene pointed. There was that silent conference between the deputies again, then they both started forward. Their feet made almost no noise on the gravel. I could see that Sergeant Blake had his gun out.

"Mr. Wagner? This is Sergeant Blake of the Gotham County Sheriff's Department. Could you come out here? We'd like to talk to you," Sergeant John Blake said.

He and Fayrene were standing on each side of the

door, their backs pressed against the side of the Winnebago, and it suddenly occurred to me that they were—not expecting, precisely, but *planning* against the possibility that Larry would choose to come out armed and shooting.

"Who's there?" I could hear Larry's voice faintly even from where I stood.

"This is Sergeant Blake from the Sheriff's Department, Mr. Wagner. Could you step outside for a moment, please?"

"Philly?" The door swung open, and there Larry stood in all his sweatshirted and fatigue-painted glory. He came down the steps looking for Maidjene, and only then saw the deputies.

"What's going on?" Larry bleated.

"Could you keep your hands away from your sides, Mr. Wagner?" Fayrene asked, with steel courtesy.

There was enough light coming from the open doorway for me to see his face go slack when he realized that, beyond all expectations and nightmares, this was *real.*

Beside me, I heard Maidjene sob as between them Blake and Fayrene had Larry turned and spread and patted down before he could figure out quite what to say.

He was lucky he wasn't armed. But he wasn't, and when they found that out the tension eased. Nobody seemed to be going to shoot anyone today, so I headed over. Maidjene followed.

I didn't think Larry was the shooter—not really—but like Maidjene said, I knew he always traveled with a number of handguns. Had he given one—intentionally or un-—to whoever'd popped Reece Wheeler?

"Where've you been for the last half hour, Mr. Wagner?"

"Was anybody with you?"

"Did anybody see you come back here?"

"Who'd you talk to today?"

"Can I take a look inside your RV, Mr. Wagner?"

Larry's head ping-ponged back and forth as the questions came at him. He fumbled through some answers, but as I watched, I realized that Blake and Fayrene didn't care as much about the answers as they did about the reaction to the questions.

"What's this about?" Larry asked, when they finally let him. "Philly? You all right?"

"A man's been shot, Mr. Wagner," Sergeant Blake said, "and we were hoping you could help us figure out who did it."

Larry stared helplessly at Maidjene. I watched her, seeing her soften, because even if the breech between them was permanent, it wasn't solid yet.

"He wasn't up there at the Circle," Maidjene said softly. "I would have seen him. He wasn't there."

"Do you have a gun, Mr. Wagner?" Sergeant Blake asked.

Larry did. Larry, in fact, had several. The deputies didn't like that much, and when he brought them out they confiscated all of them, tipping them into evidence bags. Blake and Fayrene'd seemed to have had the same idea I had, and the guns were going down to the main office for testing.

And so was Larry, apparently.

"Just a formality, Mr. Wagner. You're going to need to make a statement."

Sergeant Blake went back inside with him while Larry got his jacket and wallet. While he was in there, the ambulance containing Reece Wheeler came slowly down the hill and headed off for the local hospital, lights silently flashing.

Maidjene was crying quietly.

"Mrs. Wagner," Fayrene said gently, "why don't you go

back to the barn and rest? There isn't anything you can do here."

"Come on, Maidjene," I said, and took her arm.

Despite the Gotham County Sheriff's Department's best efforts at crowd control, people were spread out all over the Paradise Lake Campground. It was a lot harder now than it had been this morning to find a quiet place to take statements, and it would have been impossible if almost everyone here hadn't already been through it once.

The patrol car with Arnold the Shotgun Man came gliding, shark-smooth, down the road while Maidjene and I were walking up. A few paces further on we ran into Bailey, and I handed Maidjene over to him.

"They're taking Larry down to the station to talk to him," I told Bailey.

"Hope they fry the ratfucker," Bailey said, and his voice was so amiable it took me a moment to realize what he'd said. "C'mon, Maidjene."

I went back toward the parking lot.

Fayrene's car, driven by somebody in uniform, passed me on the way, and when I got back down to the lot, Sergeant Blake and Larry were just getting into it.

"You just bring that back here in one piece, you hear me, John-Boy?" Fayrene said. Blake waved, and backed it around.

I closed the distance between me and Fayrene.

"I do hate amateurs with guns," she said to me.

"So do I," I said feelingly. There was a pause while I remembered something else I had to do. "About those registration forms?" I said. I tried not to look toward the Snake's van and twitched instead, body language I somehow suspected Fayrene would have no trouble reading.

"A little bird told me that we were going to have some trouble getting those after this evening. I truly do hate to lay paper on Mrs. Wagner, but I'm not sure she's giving us a lot of choice."

I hesitated. Fayrene had obviously heard that the forms had been burned; considering that all of Summerisle knew, a leak wasn't too surprising. But of all the things Maidjene needed in her life, a subpoena wasn't one of them.

"If you could wait until Monday, probably we could work something out," I said reluctantly. Reluctantly, because I knew that tomorrow I was going to go and tell Maidjene what I'd done and try to convince her to hand the documents over freely. And if I couldn't manage that, I'd hand them over myself, but I wouldn't lie to Maidjene.

"Could we." Fayrene's voice was flat. "You sleeping down here?" she added.

"Maybe," I said. "I haven't made up my mind yet." And she hadn't told me whether I'd won my reprieve.

"What about your fella?"

It's disorienting to be on close terms with the police; they're always coming up with conversational icebreakers based on confidences you don't remember telling them.

"You mean Julian?" It's best to get these things clear. "He wanted some privacy tonight." I wondered where Julian was right now, not that I suspected him of shooting anybody.

"Hm-m." Fayrene was noncommittal. "If we wait until Monday, you are going to hand me those HallowFest forms." It was not a question.

"I will or Maidjene will," I said, and felt the weight of *intention* make my scalp tingle. As though, somewhere, *She* was listening and taking note of what I'd said.

"Mm-n," Fayrene said, letting me off the hook for now. "Is there anyplace a person can get a cup of coffee around here? Or do we have to go back and wake up Helen?"

Privately, I doubted if Helen Cooper ever slept.

"I think there's a pot on up at the barn. She told me Reverend Harm had been up here that Friday?" I asked. There was nothing wrong with checking.

"Mm-n. The way Bat figures it, Harm came back later looking for trouble. And found some. Now, about that coffee?"

"Come on."

We headed back for the barn at an ambling pace. Fayrene was content to be silent, and I had meditations of my own. The sheriff's deputies hadn't found the gun used in tonight's shooting, and conventional wisdom said that if they hadn't found it yet, the odds were good they wouldn't find it.

But what about the knife?

They hadn't found that either, and like Fayrene said, the thing that had made that hole in Reverend Harm wasn't any Buck knife. So where was it? At the bottom of Paradise Lake with the gun?

Maybe, but I doubted it. A gun is a gun is a gun, interchangeable and anonymous. Even if they found it, if they didn't have the good luck to have the bullet out of Reece Wheeler for a ballistics match, they wouldn't be able to weave a chain of evidence. But the knife, by its particular uniqueness, would retain a stronger connection to its wielder. Latent prints, occult (which is to say, *hidden*) blood, even someone, somewhere who'd remember the murderer buying it or showing it off. The wise murderer wouldn't do something as rash as simply throw it away. It could all too easily be found.

And that was only assuming this was murder most secular. Once you assumed that the murder had taken place in a ritual context, it was even more unlikely that the murderer would get rid of the knife. In most schools of magic-with-a-K, the knife—*athamé* to us Witches—is the symbol of the will, and in magic, the symbol not only

represents the thing itself, the symbol *is* the thing.
No magician would throw away his will.
So where was it?
And would I recognize it if I saw it?

Mirabile dictu, there was an actual percolator set up inside the barn. It was on a card table, and there were three boxes of Dunkin' Donuts next to it. Ragnar was standing beside the table, doughnut in one hand, the other supporting Iduna, who was slung over one shoulder like a bag of laundry, fast asleep. He was talking to a uniformed deputy, and both sets of body language told me they were meeting as equals. Hell, for all I knew Ragnar might *be* a LEO, when he wasn't being here.

It's a strange dichotomy that our Community has. Thirty years ago the counterculture was politically homogenous: liberal and left-leaning, white and upper middle class. These days there are a thousand countering cultures, and my particular slice of it—NeoPaganism— contains left- and right-wingers in about equal numbers. It would be possible, if you looked long enough, to find among us representatives from both sides of the barricades at Kent State and Chicago.

"Well, I better go put Punkin to bed. You let me know if there's anything I can do for you, Lieutenant Dix," Ragnar said, wandering off.

Fayrene drew herself a cup of coffee. So did I. I usually take it light and sweet, but tonight drinking it black seemed more appropriate.

While we were standing there, Detective Wayne came in through the front. He looked like he'd been seriously interrupted from something that he liked doing better than this, and zeroed in on the coffee by what seemed to be some kind of preconscious radar. He didn't speak until he had a cup in his hand.

"Whadda we got?"

I listened while Fayrene and Lieutenant Dix gave it to him all over again. By now I'd heard the evening's events described over and over to the point that their real-life randomness was starting to take on symmetry and meaning.

"Nothing to do with your case, Bat," Fayrene said. "They weren't even members of Harm's congregation."

"Neither was whoever shot Reece," Mad Anthony Wayne said, "but I'd sure like to have a chat with him."

"Shooters don't usually change their luck that way," Fayrene mused. It took me a moment to realize it was shorthand for: *"He probably isn't the same person who stabbed Harm, because . . ."* While I was piecing that together, she continued: "John-Boy's down at the shop taking a statement from a Lawrence Bernard Wagner, the soon-to-be-ex of the woman running this thing. Mr. Wagner came up here with a number of personal firearms and no permits."

"Did he?" Wayne said with interest.

I restrained an impulse to defend Larry. He hadn't stabbed Harm (probably), or shot Reece, and the Sheriff's Office knew it.

Probably.

"I tell you," Wayne said to nobody in particular, "I ought to shut this place down, and if one more thing happens, I will, I swear to God. Sometime tomorrow I'm going to try to get some people out here to drag the lake, and I don't want to have to do it while the Dance of the Sugarplum Fairy's going on."

I thought of mentioning that Paradise Lake'd be deserted inside of forty-eight hours anyway, but decided he didn't want to hear it. As for Sugarplum Fairies, the Transgender Ball is held at Paresis Hall in NYC, not here. I didn't mention that either.

Coffee in hand, Wayne wandered off to find someone else to talk to, and Dix went with him.

I looked at Fayrene.

"He's just cranky 'cause he doesn't think we're going to get this one. I think he's right," Fayrene said. "It's looking like anybody could've helped himself to one of Mr. Wagner's guns," she added in disgust, which was about as close as she was going to come to leveling with me.

In fiction we'd unbosom ourselves to each other and become fast allies with a *simpatica* that transcended job barriers. I would become her trusted eyes and ears in the NeoPagan Community, and she'd become my judiciary *imprimatur,* to be wielded at will once I'd scoped out the villain. But this was reality, and things didn't work that way—at least I was pretty sure they didn't. There was no reason for Fayrene to suddenly treat me as her equal. For all she could know, *I'd* popped Jackson Harm.

"So what do you think?" Fayrene said to me.

I shrugged. "I think it would help to know *why* Jackson Harm was killed." Never mind that if you know *how* you know *who,* to quote Lord Peter; if I knew *why* I'd be able to make a better guess at the killer.

Take a stab at it, so to speak.

Fayrene blew out a long sigh. "It would that, not that we're likely to ever know. We won't have the complete autopsy report until next week, but the M.E. can tell now there wasn't any unusual trauma. Our boy just lay down and took it like a man."

"Did he come here to meet somebody?" I asked, because whether she'd tell me or not, I was curious.

"When you find out, you let us know. You take care of yourself now, Bast."

I was dismissed.

The rest of the evening, like so much of life, was anticlimax. The deputies pulled out in increments, still without finding—so gossip ran—either the shootist or the shooting iron. A couple of people got to join Larry down at the station to make extended statements. I wondered if Bat Wayne would get his wish and be able to drag the lake tomorrow, and if so, what he'd find.

Some determined people went back up to the bonfire to have a Bardic Circle in spite of everything, but I wasn't one of them. I'd gone to the interrupted ritual for a healing and relinking that'd gotten overtaken by events, and I felt peculiarly unconnected from the warp of myth and deity in which I usually spend my life. There wasn't, as the headshrinkers say, *closure.* The evening felt unfinished, though considering how it had started, maybe that was a blessing.

And Jackson Harm was still dead.

The whole campground was alive with the separate lights of various tents—all battery operated, because of the fire regs. The fire at the Bardic Circle was plainly visible from lakeside. I prowled around for a while and finally found Lark.

He was sitting on the edge of the party that had gathered around Ironshadow's tent with a guitar on his knees and a bottle by his ankle and for just a heartbeat it was forever ago and none of us would ever grow old.

"Yo, Bast," he said, looking up. I knelt down beside him.

Across the party, I could see Ironshadow holding court under the tent awning, the usual ladies-in-waiting around him in long skirts or embroidered jeans. I wondered if I could brace him for backup when I faced Maidjene. Doing that was something I wasn't looking forward to, but the alternative was forfeiting my own good opinion of myself. And I was willing to go through a lot to avoid that.

"You feeling better?" Lark asked tentatively.

"Oh, sure, getting rousted by weasels with weapons and then doing the masochism tango with our friends the police sets me up real good," I shot back without thinking.

"Hey," Lark said, with only a little edge to it, "I thought you *liked* the police."

I looked up at him. The unwavering lantern light left his face half in shadow, the brights and darks making it hard to read.

I thought about it. "Not really. I like justice."

"Justice." Now Lark sounded definitely bitter. He handed the guitar off to someone else, who took it willingly and began to retune it. He picked up the bottle and stood up. "Go for a walk?" he asked. I walked with Lark away from the lantern light, out between the oases of parties.

"You still living in that place in Brooklyn?" he asked.

I remembered the place in Brooklyn, though it's been about ten years. It'd overlooked Fort Hamilton Park and there'd been six of us living there, some of us running away, some of us running to. More than the apartment, I remembered the bed, which had been lumpy and untrustworthy and had tended to collapse at inopportune moments. I remembered Lark.

"No; I got Van's old place when he moved back to Ohio." Common friends, common history. I slid my arm around his waist. Lark had muscles I didn't remember from the last time I'd seen him. I wondered what changes the years had wrought in Lark's body. I wondered if I was going to be self-destructive enough to try and find out.

"What? That coffin down in Alphabet City?"

This was unfair. My apartment is bigger than a coffin, though not by much, and it's several blocks north of Alphabet City. At least five.

"Yeah." And would Lark have looked so attractive if there hadn't been Julian? Was Lark my anodyne to that sweet nepenthe? And who would be my antidote to Lark when that time came?

"Damn if it's big enough for two. Too bad; I'm kind of looking for a place to crash for a while," Lark said regretfully. "You know of anybody with crash space?"

Once I'd been younger, with infinite optimism and resource. In those days I would have invited Lark to move in with me anyway, certain that rising above the cramped inconvenience would be an adventure. I am older now and no longer certain there is that much generosity of spirit anywhere in the world.

"Maybe Belle," I said, thinking it over. Belle has four bedrooms and a landlord she likes to annoy with the specter of illegal sublets. "I can ask her."

"But you're not in Changing anymore," Lark said, as if I needed reminding. "That going to make a difference?" I thought again about what Glitter had said; that Belle was going to give up the coven, and that she might let me use her space to run one of my own. If I started one, something that looked more likely by the moment.

"It was an amicable separation," I said dryly. "And you can ask her yourself if you'd rather."

"Not me," Lark said hastily. "You do it, okay?"

"Yeah, sure," I said. It wouldn't make any difference, and I thought Belle would probably do it. I wondered just how Lark was planning to keep himself in cigarettes and gasoline while he was here; when I'd known him last he'd been working in a bookstore, but that had been in the eighties and we'd all been pretending we didn't want to be yuppies.

Of course, *I* was still doing what *I'd* been doing in the eighties.

Behind us, the guitarist swung into the opening chords of Gwyddion's "We Won't Wait Any Longer," that confrontational marching song of the (Not Very) Old Religion.

"So, what do you think's going to happen to us?" Lark said. It took me a moment to realize that Lark was using "us" in the greater cosmic sense—i.e., the attendees of HallowFest.

"Nothing much," I said. "They'd like to find the gun that townie got shot with." *And I'd like to find the knife Jackson Harm got stabbed with, come to that.* "But they don't have much in the way of suspects."

Lark sneered. "You don't have to be a weatherman to know which way the wind blows," he misquoted. "They'd rather it was one of us. They'll look till they find out it is."

City people are sometimes surprised at how fast the United States turns redneck, once you're outside of the major population centers. And anyone with half a brain can see that the winds of change are blowing very cold on the fringes of society these days. While it hasn't yet gotten to the point that difference itself is a criminal act, I wondered how many things were being assumed about us by the Gotham County natives on the basis of the knives we carried and the clothes we wore. Which prejudgment is not in and of itself an uncommon act, but usually the stakes aren't as high as murder.

Lark put his arm across my shoulders and offered me the bottle. I stopped and tilted it back—Ironshadow mead and worth the trip all by itself. I drank and passed it back, and Lark drank. We walked on. His arm was still around me.

"So who's that guy you came up here with?"

"Julian?"

Was Lark jealous? Flattering if true, but I was smart enough to know that it probably wasn't Lark I wanted, really, so much as the gilded past we'd shared.

And what about Julian? Gratifying to think of having the need to choose between them, if unlikely.

"He runs the Snake—the Serpent's Truth; that big occult bookstore down in—"

"I've heard of it," Lark said. "Didn't it get bombed last year?"

"Something like that," I said. "It happens a lot." Which is true, actually.

"And nobody cares—because it's us. If it was one of us got popped up here, do you think the cops'd be running around like headless chickens trying to pin it on somebody?"

"Now that you mention it, yes. That's what they do. Pin things on people. Usually on the ones who did them."

We stopped again. Lark drank. He passed the bottle over to me conscientiously, but we were on the edge of an argument all the same.

"Come on," I said. "Let's go back."

He grunted noncommitally but turned around. His fingers dug into my shoulder, even through my parka and sweater, as if he'd forgotten I was there.

"How long are you going to stick up for them?" Lark demanded, and although it's a clichéd question, it sounded like he really wanted to know.

"Some things are right, Lark, and some aren't . . ." I waffled.

"And so it doesn't matter who you've got on the same side as you, so long as they're right?"

It sounded logical, but not the way he put it. "No. I mean, yes." He always could confuse me. "You know that—"

"You don't know what you're talking about," Lark said flatly. Irrationally, that irritated me more than any other sort of insult might have. I pulled away from him. He let me go.

"See you later," I said, walking away fast before either of us could say anything else.

I stopped at some other parties, ingested an alarming array of mixed drinks, and tried not to brood too much. Nobody mentioned Harm's murder; in fact, even tonight's shooting incident wasn't the main topic of conversation. In fact, it was a Saturday night much like other Saturday nights at other HallowFests. I was the thing that had

changed. I was seeing these people—my kin, my clan—
the way an outsider would; and the more I realized that
the problem came from within me, the more irritated I was
with them. Over and over I found myself judging my fellow festival attendees as if I were seeing them for the first
time. It wasn't a comfortable mindset.

Eventually I wound up back by Ironshadow's tent.
Lark had moved on, so I stuck there for a while. Ironshadow gave me my own bottle of home brew, and I took
it down a couple of inches chasing homemade beer and
damiana wine and even some authentic absinthe, brewed
from a recipe that *Scientific American* published (in its innocence) a few years back.

The company was good and the mead was better and
the guitar was playing Richard Thompson and Mike Long-
cor and the works of other cute guys with beards. But my
thoughts weren't pleasant company—for me or anyone
else around Ironshadow's tent—so after a while I left
there, too.

On my way down to my cold and lonely pallet in the
back of Julian's van I noticed that every light in the barn
was on, even the ones upstairs, where nobody was supposed to be right now. Maybe I wasn't the only one who
felt the uneasiness in the air, as though the dead who
were supposed to ride three weeks from now had come
through the Gate Between the Worlds early and stalked
among us now without our knowledge.

The parking area seemed cold and deserted after the
Lake Meadow, but I was still full of Ironshadow mead, and
between the packing quilts and my sleeping bag and the
fact that the human body, left to itself, can radiate quite
enough heat to warm even as uninsulated a space as the
inside of the van, I certainly wouldn't freeze. I pulled the
doors shut behind me and locked them. There was no real
point to getting undressed; I pulled off my boots but left
my parka on this time. After all, my friend Lace sleeps in

her leather jacket even at home, so she tells me; I didn't feel too far outside the normative curve.

And, I thought with woozy romanticism, if Julian wanted privacy for ritual, a certain fellow-feeling and noblesse oblige required I give it to him. Too many of us have too little safe space in our lives for ritual, and I could not manage to begrudge it to anyone, even if it did leave me sleeping in the parking lot.

I did not worry about a lot of things that I ought, in retrospect, have worried about, from improbabilities such as being murdered in the van to the likelihood of more nightmares. I didn't worry about what Lark was thinking of me and I didn't even worry about my relationship with Julian, or about what ritual he was doing—and why.

I went to sleep.

7

I knew exactly what time it was because my wristwatch glows in the dark. What I didn't know was why I was awake, soberly and completely, out of a dreamless, alcohol-assisted slumber.

A gunshot?

It was possible that something like that could have awakened me without my remembering hearing it. I did not want to think of what, other than a loud noise, could have done it; psychic summonses and other staples of occult literature, while part of my worldview, tended to lead to rendezvous even less pleasant than those heralded by gunfire.

What was a fact was that I wasn't going back to sleep. So I could either sit here in the dark for three hours until sunrise, read while running down the van's already weak battery, or find some other way of amusing myself.

I found the flashlight and turned it on. It failed after I'd found my boots but before I got them on. I groped my way out of the back of the van by touch. It was colder outside than in; no surprise.

Once on my feet and reconciled to insomnia, I tried to look on the bright side of things. It was my favorite time of night, and a time that I, being a freelancer able to set my own hours, see more often than not, when that part of night that begins with sunset has run its course and the part that's a dry run for dawn hasn't started. The bowl of night; the unchanging moment in a world of change. It was calm (wind is a part of dawn) and dark, and very nearly quiet.

And now at last I felt what I'd searched for in vain earlier this evening. The breath of the Goddess on the back of my neck; the immanence of deity. It was a good feeling—the security that children leave behind in childhood, that adults have left on the barricades of the Industrial Revolution; an incontrovertible sense of belonging to a world that is complete and whole. It was a gift, and such gifts demand reciprocation. What gift could I make in return?

I knew the answer to that, but the question really was, what gift was I *willing* to make?

I started up the path to the barn, but I didn't end up going to the barn. It was dark, full of sleeping Pagans, and it wasn't my destination anyway. Julian's cabin was dark, too—Registration, at the other end of the row, was the lone light, and I didn't have the feeling there was anyone awake there, either.

I remembered other HallowFests, where three A.M. would not have meant silence and darkness, where the Bardic Circle had lasted until dawn and we'd cooked breakfast over the embers of the fire. But that was long ago and in a far decade, and those Pagans had changed—gone on to other paths, or just grown up.

It struck me with a sudden unwelcome force that of my circle of NeoPagan friends and Aquarian acquaintance from the early eighties, I was almost the only one left. Van was dead, Thomas had left us for the Christians, Belle was about to retire, others had moved on, grown up, gotten out. *"And I alone am escaped to tell thee . . ."* I felt

the same sort of spooky embarrassment that you feel
when you've just realized you've stayed too long at the
party. It was time for me to move on, too—talk to Belle,
talk to Lark, take the next step of becoming teacher and
leader.

But if I did that, someday that would end, too. That
was the underlying truth of what I was resisting; change
is a movement forward in time, and everyone knows that
such movement someday ends.

Or, as in the Reverend Harm's case, is ended prema-
turely.

I circled around the cabins, and then around the lake.
I had no particular destination in mind; eventually I might
go up to the bonfire. There'd be people there; someone always kept firewatch until the embers were cold. But I
wasn't really looking for people.

I thought. Until I heard the voices.

I was across the near side of the meadow that sur-
rounds the lake, off into an area that's slowly being taken
over by second-growth timber. People camp there some
years, but the prime camping area is around the lake, and
this year everyone had been accommodated there.

"Life is pain."

I could make out what they were saying about the
same time I saw the light—closer than was really prudent,
but rocks and straggling bushes had concealed the area.
Which was one of the reasons they'd chosen it, of course.

"Pain is truth."

It was a tiny fire; mostly charcoal on a bed of sand in
something that looked like an institutional-size wok.
Something that would leave no trace in the morning's
light. There were candles in hurricane lamps at three
points, putting the wok-fire in the center of a triangle.

"Truth is life."

Xharina was standing in the ritual space, across from
one of her coveners, wearing a black corset that offered

up her bare breasts like cupcakes, and a long skirt that looked like it was made of animal tails. Her tattoos gave her arms a mottled motile surface as though they were wreathed in snakes. She was holding a knife in her hand.

It wasn't one of Ironshadow's polite carriage-trade *athamés* with the maidenly double-sided six-inch blade. Xharina was holding a point-heavy single-edge Bowie knife with an eleven-inch blade. It flashed like a mirror in the firelight, and leather tails were braided over the hilt, ending in a tassel as long as hilt and blade together. She held the flat of the blade to the flames for a moment.

One of her coveners—Arioch, I think, though I wasn't sure—was standing opposite her. He was bare to the waist, wearing jeans that were black or leather or both.

Xharina cut him.

She started just above the nipple and cut careful diagonal marks into his pectoral muscle—they'd look like the marks of the Sioux Sun Dance when they healed. She pulled the blade along slowly, painstakingly, like a child trying her best to color inside the lines, and I could hear Arioch first catch his breath, then breathe slowly and raggedly, as if what he was feeling were not pain. She cut six lines, evenly spaced, working from bottom to top so that the surface she was working on was always dry.

"I am the shadow where three roads meet; I am the durable fire. I am the night-howling dog; the mortal wound of love; the madness of fear; and the exercise of power. I am mastery and desire, and all roads lead to me. I am the sword in the hand; I am the scars on the soul. I am the whip that drives you; I am the flesh beneath the lash. I am the shadow where three roads meet—"

Against the sound of Xharina's voice the others murmured an antiphon, too low for me to hear. Arioch's head was thrown back, in a gesture I'd have difficulty not recognizing as ecstasy, but other than that he had not moved.

I should not be here. I'd stumbled into a mystery of which I was not initiate; the worship of a more primordial Mother than the aspect my tradition's rituals courted. The power raised here was rawly seductive; gooseflesh hackled on my skin and I felt as if someone had opened the door of a blast furnace in my face.

Xharina dabbled her fingers in the blood and wrote the sign of the horns on Arioch's forehead with it. He knelt, and she stepped around the fire to approach him. I used the cover of their movement to get away, hoping they hadn't seen me.

I was more intent on distance than destination; the next thing I knew I was down by Mrs. Cooper's house, along the road that led to the outside world. My heart was pounding as if I'd run to get here; I was flushed and shaking, and once again, like an unwanted guest, I could feel the projected outrage of the outsider inside my skin.

But what Xharina and her people were doing was not wrong by any standard—Goddess knew it was consensual. I'd seen Arioch with Xharina before; nothing in the way he acted indicated that he was someone trapped in a ritual relationship that had gone wrong in any of the many ways those intimate relationships can. Arioch had been happy where he was yesterday, and would still be happy tomorrow morning.

I believed it; I had felt no threat when I'd accidentally stumbled into their ritual. But the outsider in my skin wasn't convinced. People don't cut people, people don't hit people because they love them.

Yes they do, I told the inside Outsider. Yes, there was blood, and yes, Xharina had cut him—but it had been done with love, and was not, when all was said and done, so much more abhorrent than the accepted practices of more established faiths. Xharina's coven's was a shamanic tradition—nothing more.

But it was so far from the self-perceived norm of Neo-

Paganism that I began to understand why Xharina's people were so skittish about networking with the rest of us. The greatest taboo in the Gardnerian-derived traditions is to allow blood to touch the ritual blade — Craft tradition holds that such a blade must be destroyed at once, and a new one consecrated. But Xharina's coveners must blood their blades regularly, if what I'd inadvertently witnessed tonight was any indication.

All unwelcome the malicious monkey part of my mind demanded attention, assuring me that those who were willing to cut shallowly could cut deeply as well — and that Reverend Harm had died of a knife wound.

They had no motive! I told myself sharply, as irritated as if some stranger had made the suggestion. And it was true — Hoodoo Lunchbox had never been to Paradise Lake before; this was their first HallowFest. They could certainly not have had any previous exposure to Reverend Harm.

But if I were going to pardon shamanism, my mind insisted, surely I should admit that human sacrifice was a part of magic as well?

Fortunately this was too ridiculous for even me to take seriously; it broke the spell of my overheated internal monologue. It was a long way from a little shamanic bloodletting to murder; you might as rationally accuse a cigarette smoker of being a pyromaniac. Yet the fact remained that Harm had been ritually murdered. Or, I thought again, had been made to *seem* to be ritually murdered, because once I had ruled out magic and religion I could imagine no nonsecular motive strong enough to actually motivate the deed.

I knew where I wanted to go, now.

It was hard to reach the pine forest without crossing the Upper Meadow where the Bardic Circle was, but I managed it by dint of a long detour and a scramble up the steep slope I'd avoided yesterday. If there was a deputy posted up here I didn't see him, but there was no reason for him to be standing right over the murder site, after all.

We were almost out of the bowl of night, now; in less than an hour there would be hints of dawn in the sky.

I'd dreamed this, I realized suddenly. I was standing in the forest, just where I had been when I'd seen Miriam. Ahead of me—toward the Circle—I could see the "Police Line—Do Not Cross" tape glowing brightly yellow in the reflected light of the fire in the meadow below. The firelight edged the downward slope sharply, giving me the illusion of enough light to see by.

Here was the last place Jackson Harm had come to alive. He'd met his killer here, and died.

It took a bit of casting about to find the exact spot where the body had been. The police don't outline victims' bodies in white paint the way you see in the *Naked Gun* movies. But I'd been here three times, under circumstances which enforce the vividness—if not the accuracy—of memory, and I found the likely spot eventually. There was a short stake with a bit of red ribbon tied to it stuck down into the forest mulch; I didn't remember seeing it before, but probably the Sheriff's Department had left it to mark the site.

I knelt down, the way I had . . . was it only this morning? I tried to still myself and open myself, and do what good divination does, allowing myself to see what there was here to see. I touched my fingers to the ground where Harm had been. *Tell me who killed you. Tell me why.*

I felt a chill reasonless excitement; the adrenaline rush that comes before the conscious mind understands the reason for it.

There was a sound.

It brought me out of half-trance like a slap in the face; it was a real-world sound; the sound of a broken twig and someone trying to shuffle quietly through the dark. I

jerked to my feet, and all I could think of was that I was
guilty of trespassing and about to be caught.

But I wasn't the only one.

"Uh . . . hi," Wyler Pascoe said.

I could just make him out in the darkness; a teenaged
blob of light and dark, identifiable mostly by the T-shirt
I'd seen him wearing yesterday at the diner. Wyler Pascoe. Sergeant Fayrene Pascoe's underage son.

"What are you doing here?" I said. It wasn't particularly gracious as opening gambits go, but he'd scared me.
And now that I'd had time to think about the consequences of his being here, I wasn't any less worried.

He made an inarticulate gesture—at least it might
have been inarticulate and was certainly a gesture. I
couldn't see him very well. The fire was not as bright as
it had been at its height, and was at the bottom of the hill
besides; most of what I could make out of Wyler was his
pale skin and pale hair and the glinting silver pentagram
he wore around his neck. I couldn't remember whether
it'd been there in the diner or not.

We didn't need this. I didn't need this. *HallowFest*
didn't need this.

"Uh . . ." Possibly Wyler wasn't sure himself. "Hey,
you're Bast, right?"

"Right." I thought about heavy-metal gangstas and
rock music Satanists and that Wyler seemed to be out
pretty late for a boy whose mother, presumably, knew the
worst that Gotham County had to offer. I thought about
the fact that Wyler probably knew Jackson Harm by sight
and could easily have gotten close to him, and that mur-
derers get younger every day, and that here he was, now,
at the scene of the crime—or back at it.

Of course, so was I.

"Is there something we can do for you here, Wyler?" I
said, in my best customer service tones.

He looked from me to the fire, much as if he was missing an appointment he longed to keep.

"I came to be a Witch!" he blurted out.

I shook my head; not at him. At the situation, if at anything, and the fact that life goes on.

"No!" Wyler protested. "I really did. I just wanted— I just thought that . . ." He stopped.

"Everybody's asleep," I said pointlessly.

"No they aren't. Not down at the bonfire. Mom was saying that there'd be somebody up by that all night, and I just thought . . ." He shrugged again.

"There'd be somebody you could talk to?" I suggested.

I walked back toward the edge of the forest, where the light was better. Wyler followed.

"Yeah," he breathed. "Mom doesn't understand, you know? She says it's just a passing phase, and if it isn't, I can look into it when I'm older. But I'm old *now*," Wyler added, with the exasperation of the sixteen-year-old self-perceived adult. "And I want to be a Witch. I've always wanted to be a Witch."

"What do you think a Witch is?" I asked him gently, part of me remembering that this was one of the first questions Belle had asked me nearly fifteen years ago.

Wyler stared at me; a good kid, I theorized from limited experience, trying hard to bring an honest answer out of the inarticulateness of teenagerhood.

"Is there somebody up there?" It was a shout from below, nervous and belligerent; one of the people on firewatch. I recollected sharply that the last people heading toward the fire from this direction had been armed, and there was still a gun unaccounted for among my fellow happy campers.

"It's me," I called down. "It's Bast." Hoping it was somebody I knew.

"Oh, hi, Bast." A new voice: Bailey of Summerisle,

thank the Goddess; someone who knew me. "We heard voices?" he went on.

"I'm up here with a friend of mine," I said mendaciously. I walked forward and looked down the slope. Bailey and a couple of other members of Summerisle were standing around the fire, looking up toward me.

"You're not really supposed to be on that side of the tape," Bailey said apologetically.

"Yeah," I said. "We're coming down. C'mon, Wyler."

No one else at the Festival knew that Wyler was Fayrene's son, and probably neither Bailey nor I knew everyone here this weekend on sight. Wyler could easily be taken for one of the campers; there wouldn't be any immediate awkward questions.

I was prepared to drag Wyler along with me by force, but apparently he'd already imprinted on me and followed, agreeable as a duckling, as I led him across the Upland Meadow and through the sleeping campground toward the parking lot.

Along the way I learned that he'd ridden over here on his bike, which he'd left down on Route 6; that he'd always wanted to be a Witch but hadn't known that was what it was called; that he'd attended Reverend Harm's Bible Summer Camp once when he was younger; and that he'd been reading as much as he could find on the subject of Wicca but that the Tamerlane Association Library wasn't much use.

"And it's what I want! I want to worship the Goddess — I *belong* to the Goddess," Wyler said.

We'd reached the parking lot by this time and didn't have to talk in whispers. Wyler glanced skyward, but at this point in the night and her cycle, Lady Moon had set long ago.

The most I'd been planning to do was drive him home

and forgo the lecture on prudence he probably deserved and wouldn't listen to. It was that gesture, I think, that convinced me to help him get what he wanted, even knowing full well his mother the deputy sheriff wouldn't be best pleased.

"Okay, look," I said. I stopped and turned to face him. "Here's the deal. You go home and don't come back."

"But—" Wyler said, drawing breath to argue.

"While the Festival is on," I said over his protest. "You do that, and I will pick out a basic Wiccan reading list for you to start on—some of the same books I started with. You come here Monday, pick up the books, and pay for them—before noon, which is when the Festival will be over and we'll be gone. Everything else you've got to square with your mom. She's got my home address, if she wants you to be in touch with me."

I watched him argue with himself over whether he could get a better deal elsewhere; whether I was being straight with him or just trying to blow him off. Kids today are so suspicious.

"I want to join a coven," Wyler said in a small strangled voice.

"I know," I said, as gently as I could. Fayrene was going to kill me, no doubt about it. "But it'll be two years before you're eighteen and can even join an Outer Court"—the pre-Initiation study and training group that most traditions use—"and you'd still have to read the books"—though every tradition's reading list is slightly different. "This way—if you want—you can practice as a solitary."

There are some people—not many, as the position is even more Old Guard than some of the ones I hold—who'd say that what I was doing now was proselytizing, something strictly forbidden to the Hidden Children of the Goddess. There were others who'd say that by selling

Wyler the books I was selling training, something as disgraceful as being a fee-charging literary agent.

But the look on Wyler's face when I held out even that prosaic hope was enough to show me that I was far too late to proselytize; he already belonged to Our Lady and he'd train himself, just as we all do. There's no central regulating body that can compel you to magical discipline; you either have it and stay or you burn out and leave.

I tell myself.

"I can be a Witch?" Wyler said.

"You're a Pagan right now if you say you are," I pointed out. "If you want to be a Witch you need coven training and initiation, but you can be a Goddess-worshipper without that. I'll give you a catalog, too—you can order more books mail order." And maybe Belle had brought some copies of Changing's introductory reading list up with her that I could swipe to tell him which ones those ought to be.

Wyler hesitated, plainly afraid he was being sold a bill of goods. "Are they very expensive—the books?" he finally said. "I don't have very much money."

"What can you afford?" I said, trying to remember if Julian had brought any copies of *What Witches Do* by Stewart Farrar up to the festival with him. When I'd come in to the Craft, it had been one of the handful of accurate books available, and I still liked it for unsensationalized descriptions of Wiccan practice and the fact that it didn't promise its readers a lot of cheap New Age miracles.

Wyler hesitated again.

"Look," I said. "I'll put together the books I think you should have in the order you ought to buy them. You come on Monday and buy whatever you want."

Wyler relaxed—Goddess knew what kind of Florida beachfront scam he'd been expecting me to field him.

"And can I buy an *athamé*, too?" he said. He pronounced it "ar-thaim," which gave me some idea of the kind of books he'd been reading so far.

"Start with the books," I said. "You can save up for an Ironshadow blade later." I would have been willing to *give* him a blade—a gift to ghosts of my own—but I couldn't afford to buy one of Ironshadow's and I didn't think the Snake's HallowFest inventory included any. Even Julian knew there wasn't a lot of point to bringing knives, with Ironshadow dealing cutlery at the next table at one-third the price. "Now get in the van. I'll run you home."

And hope Fayrene hadn't noticed he was gone, or I'd have to do a lot more explaining than I wanted to just now. Or ever, if I had my choice.

We stopped back on Route 6 to pick up Wyler's bike—it was carefully chained to a road sign, which struck me as slightly ridiculous—and then I pulled a three-point turn (traffic at fourish A.M. in Gotham County is nonexistent) and headed in the direction of Tamerlane and Wyler's home address. At least if I saw him into the house I could swear to Fayrene later that I'd brought him home.

Home, for Wyler and Sergeant Fayrene Pascoe both, turned out to be a double-wide in the Hidden Valley trailer park—lower-middle-income's answer to the high cost of new housing and the higher cost of upkeep in the Northeast. The sky was perceptibly light by the time I got there, and out of the corner of my eye I could see Wyler fidgeting nervously.

"What time does your mom get up in the morning?" I asked.

"She's on nights now," Wyler said. "She gets home about six."

Which explained how he'd come to be over at Paradise Lake.

"But sometimes she gets home earlier," Wyler added mournfully.

I pulled carefully into the entrance of the park, past the bank of ganged mailboxes that looked like some bizarre form of birdhouse. The road curved around the park in a horseshoe fashion with trailers parked on both sides of it—pink and white or beige and brown, with the odd-man-out aluminum Airstream hitch-trailer. The trailers in the center backed on each other, but the ones on the outside of the U had nothing behind them but the scrub woods and ACREAGE FOR SALE signs that edged most of County 6.

I drove slowly down the serried ranks. The plots of grass beside the trailers ran heavily to yellow plastic daisy windspinners and foot-high preformed plastic picket fences. There were lawn chairs and barbecue grills and occasional forsaken children's toys. Most of the trailers' windows were still dark, but even at this hour—I checked my watch, 5:15—lights were on here and there.

At Wyler's direction I pulled into the asphalted parking spot beside a white trailer that looked more like a house than some of the others here. If Fayrene was home she was keeping quieter about it than I would in the same circumstances.

"Got your key?" I asked Wyler.

He gave me a funny look. "It isn't locked," he said, as if that were something everyone should know.

I left the van idling as Wyler slid out of the passenger seat. We got his bike out of the back; he propped it against the side of the trailer and bounced up the steps—it wasn't locked, as he'd said—and a moment later returned to wave me an "all clear."

I got back into the van and backed carefully out of the space. The secret of his midnight visit was safe with him, but that was no guarantee I wouldn't hear about it from Fayrene—one thing that experience has taught me is that most people give up their secrets far too easily. I reached Route 6 again and turned left, leaving behind me the housing made of ticky-tacky that all looked just the same.

When I was younger Life was simpler—I could have guilt-lessly deplored the entire dehumanizing idea of living in a trailer park in the low-income housing enforced conformity of the blue-collar yahoo who existed only to destroy my own infinitely more interesting slacker demographic. I could have waxed lyrical on how life in a trailer park was a living death, creating an army of *volkskultur*-ingesting Eloi who were a threat but not of interest, and on how I, through sheer puissant superiority, would forever evade such a fate.

I still thought most of those things—well, some of them, anyway—but I'd ceased to believe that living in a New York City apartment was some index of moral superiority. Maybe I was wiser now, or maybe just tired; the main thing that struck me about Hidden Valley trailer park was that it must be nice to live somewhere you trusted your neighbors enough to retain the old country habit of not locking your doors at night.

And then again, maybe they just knew that anyone could get into one of those things with a large screwdriver and an unkind word, so why bother?

I hate seeing both sides of every question.

Mom's Diner was on my way back to Paradise Lake. I almost stopped for an early breakfast before it occurred to me that Fayrene was probably in there right now, and that the last thing I actually wanted was to have to explain to her what I was doing out here in the real world instead of safely tucked up in my comforting fantasy.

I was no fit company for man nor beast, anyway. Or for woman or deputy, for that matter.

The sun was well up and the day was getting started when I slipped the Snake's van back into its parking place at Paradise Lake. This time I had no trouble falling asleep.

8

SUNDAY, OCTOBER 8—10:30 A.M.

The next time I woke up it was to the sound of slamming doors. I looked at my watch. Ten-thirty, and I had the feeling I'd been supposed to open the Snake's table about half an hour ago.

I jammed on my boots and opened the back door of the van. The day was bright; at least we'd been blessed with good weather this weekend.

Xharina was leaving.

Both back doors and the side were open on the black van with the flaming guitar painted on the side, and boxes and guitars were being loaded with a speed and skill that suggested this activity was one that Hoodoo Lunchbox performed frequently.

I didn't see Arioch anywhere. The events of the previous night came back to me suddenly, vivid with the immediacy of memory, and I found myself flushing.

Xharina turned and saw me. After that, I couldn't just walk away pretending I hadn't seen her and them without it seeming highly suspicious. Besides, it was partly at my insistence that they'd come to HallowFest at all, and I owed them common courtesy at least as much as I wanted to cover my tracks.

I went over. "You're leaving early," I said.

This morning Xharina was wearing riding breeches—
the old kind that are tight to the knee and have the
lagniappe of fabric at the thighs—with her paddock boots
and a sleeveless black silk camp shirt. Her tats burned
jelly-jar bright in the sunlight. I still wondered how Xharina, being Xharina, managed to walk in footgear with
heels that low.

"This isn't exactly the kind of place we belong," Xharina said tactfully. "So we thought we'd cut our losses."

So to speak.

Arioch appeared, leaning out of the van to take something from one of the others. He was wearing a white T-
shirt under his vest this morning, and I was almost sure
I could spot the bulk of a thick gauze dressing under the
tee. He saw me and grinned.

I felt myself lose it completely; a blind deafman would
know that I knew what he'd been doing last night. Fortunately, Arioch wasn't paying attention.

But Xharina was.

She turned her back on the others and took a step
away. I followed her.

"We were doing some ritual out in the woods last
night," she said when I reached her. I found myself unable to meet her eyes, a sensation I analyzed for its
strangeness even while it unnerved me. I took a deep
breath and held it, forcing my diaphragm muscles to
relax. I didn't think I was ashamed of either of us, and I
certainly had no desire for anyone to carve *me* with a
Bowie.

"I couldn't sleep. I was out walking last night," I said.

"And what did you think?" Xharina said. Her voice
wasn't neutral now. It was angry.

"I think what I saw wasn't any of my business," I said
honestly.

"Sure it wasn't," Xharina said bitterly. "But that isn't
going to stop you from phoning all your friends and telling

them all about it. Why not?—it isn't as though we're really Pagans or anything."

I thought of telling her that I didn't have any friends, but Xharina didn't need stand-up comedy right now. "It was a ritual. What I saw I didn't have any business seeing," I repeated. "I'm not going to tell anybody."

"And I suppose we'll just take your word for that?" Xharina said.

"What choice have you got?" I said, starting to get angry myself. "I've told you twice it was an accident—do you think I went out looking for you?"

"Maybe." Xharina looked me up and down in a way that was meant to be insolent and succeeded pretty well. "Maybe you were looking for—what we have."

There was no use denying I knew what that was, and knee-jerk denials are not my specialty anyway. With toxic fair-mindedness, I remembered waking up out of a sound sleep and going looking for . . . what? Them? I shook my head. Even if Xharina were right—and she might be—I could see no happiness for myself down that particular path, and given a choice I wouldn't walk it. There are degrees of separation from the mainstream; I could see Xharina's from where I was, but that didn't mean I wanted to go there.

"Maybe," I said reluctantly. "But I didn't mean to crash your ritual. I'm sorry."

"Okay." The word came on a sigh, an indication of how wired Xharina was. There was a pause. "Nobody else noticed," she said. "I knew there was someone but I didn't know who, and I thought . . ."

That it was Jackson Harm's killer trolling for new victims? Or something darker?

"Cheer up," I said glibly, "I'll keep my mouth shut and they'll make stuff up about you anyway."

That made her grin. Xharina wasn't averse to bad

press and living the legend—except, I realized, when there was truth to the rumors.

"I'd say you should come party with us sometime," she said, "but I don't do women. I know some people, though."

I wasn't sure whether the offer was serious or whether she was still trying to jerk my chain, and on this particular morning I wasn't even sure which I wanted it to be.

"I'll keep that in mind," I said, settling for neutral politeness. "You folks have a safe trip home."

"See you at the Snake," Xharina said, and strode back to her coven.

I took the long way up to the barn, rearranging the inside of my head into something that wouldn't get into my way and trying to push the brilliant flash of the blade in Xharina's hands back somewhere into unconsulted memory-space.

And doing that made me forget about most of what else had happened last night, too.

It was only after I got up to the barn that I realized everything I needed to have to open up the table was down in the van. By the time I got back down to the parking lot again, Hoodoo Lunchbox was gone, which was, all things considered, a relief. I was pretty sure Xharina hadn't killed Jackson Harm, but I couldn't feel as certain about her boys—jailhouse tats, biker colors, and all. There was no reason other than bloody-minded suspicion for me to think any of them *had* done it, of course, and when I faced that thought, I realized that my subconscious didn't want to pin Harm's murder on Hoodoo Lunchbox as much as on their equipment.

It was, after all, a similar case to Reece Wheeler's shooting last night—a weapon appears, is used, and vanishes again. But even disappearing knives have to come from somewhere, and I suspected that Hoodoo Lunchbox traveled with a lot of them.

Of course, so did the Klingons. I wondered where Orm Klash and his brethren and sistern were this morning.

I got the cashbox and the jewelry and a few other odds and ends and headed up for the barn.

This time I didn't miss my chance to swing by the cabins and see if Julian was there. He wasn't. I wondered which of the workshops he was attending—without the cashbox, he probably wasn't up at the dealer's table. Imagination failed. I could not imagine Julian—ascetic, cerebral Julian—engaged in any of the well-meaning anarchy of a HallowFest.

As if to underscore this, the cabin was as neat as a monk's cell, with everything folded and put away as if Julian intended to make a habit out of living here. The scent of cold incense smoke covered the cabin's mustiness with a sharp tang: frankincense, mostly, and—

And amber, cinnamon, bergamot, and myrrh—at least if Julian was following the *Tesoraria* rituals, which that silver knife he'd gotten from Ironshadow indicated he was.

Interesting, but hardly of immediate importance. Julian is a student of magic; he's nearly always engaged in some magickal operation or other. Something niggled at the back of my mind, then, but I ignored it in favor of getting set up for the day. I wondered where I'd be sleeping tonight. I didn't think I could manage another night in the back of the van.

I had customers waiting when I got upstairs and no Julian in sight, which kept me busy supplying catalogs and making change for the next half hour. Since this was Sunday, business was picking up—people had done their window-shopping yesterday and now were ready to buy. One of my customers volunteered to go downstairs and get me coffee and I bought a couple of trail-mix muffins from the bake sale table next door (chewy, but filling) and settled down at the table.

A Welsh trad named Gerry came and asked me if we had any ritual robes—he'd seen Hallie's and didn't like the informality of the tie-dye. I was sure we'd packed some on Friday, but a quick search of the boxes under the table turned up altar cloths and Tarot cloths and everything but. I promised to keep looking, and Gerry promised to come back later, and possibly both of us would keep our promises.

Business slacked off with the start of the eleven o'clock workshop. It would probably pick up again at the lunch break, and then there'd be a last go in the late afternoon before Merchanting was shut down for the night. Tomorrow there'd be no workshops; the merchants would be able to open for a couple of hours before loading to leave. The last event of the weekend would be the "opening" ritual for next year's HallowFest. The closing ritual for this year's Festival was still a year away.

Ironshadow wasn't here yet, but he'd partied hearty and late last night and had the added advantage of merchanting a small and portable stock; I supposed he'd be here when he felt like it, if he didn't just decide to deal what he had left out of his tent today instead. *I* would have, given the option; the day outside was one of those bright autumnal glories that actually make people want to live in the country with kamikaze skunks, woodlice, and attack deer. I'm a city girl, myself.

It got to be noon. I wondered how Larry's evening on the cutting edge of law enforcement had been, and tried to remember if I'd seen him around the Warwagon this morning. I wondered where Julian was, since he wasn't in the cabin and didn't seem the type to go for long nature rambles. And then, for a change of pace, I wondered why Lark hadn't come around to see me this morning. It was true we hadn't parted on the best of terms, but with Lark that didn't mean a helluva lot, unless he'd changed more than I thought. If I was even thinking about tapping him for my working partner I was going to need to know exactly where I stood with him and whether he was, in the quaint patois of Organized Crime, a "stand-up guy."

And if not Lark, who? I began going over all the males of my acquaintance who were (a) semidetached and (b) initiate Gardnerians, trying to think of who would do for me. Assuming, of course, that I would do for them. When that got frustrating enough, I looked around for something to do and realized I hadn't brought a book with me—not a problem, you'd say, since I was running a table for a bookstore, but Julian had brought up a collection of books I'd either already read or wouldn't read if the alternative were illiteracy.

He doesn't like the stock bent anyway.

So I read the more expensive of the two *Tesorarias* for a while but got bored with that too, since a grimoire's got as much plot as a cookbook—a really boring one.

Aside from its particular purpose of ending all spiritual outside influence on the petitioner, *La Tesoraria* is similar to other grimoires of the period. Its rituals require a detailed knowledge of Latin, Greek, Hebrew, and astrology, and a list of ingredients that not only keeps stores like The Snake in business but guarantees that the legitimate magician will never find himself with time or excess money on his hands. Needless to say, I am not drawn to the more esoteric reaches of Ceremonial Magic; in fact I have a suspicion that the rituals in most grimoires—like the advice in their distant cousin, the *Kama Sutra*—are mostly designed to be read and not done.

For example, at the end of working of *La Tesoraria del Oro* there are two acts the practitioner must perform. They're impossible, of course, but, like Welsh riddles, once you've gotten that far you have to solve them to finish the game. In order to receive his theurgical bill of divorcement, the petitioner, once he has completed his year of abstinence and observance, must first slay himself, and then have congress with himself—as the translated Spanish so quaintly puts it. I'd gotten that far in the read-through of the translated manuscript when I asked Julian if he had me working on the world's longest Polish terrorist joke (you know, the one that ends: "—first me, and then all of my hostages!"). He'd just given me one of those smug cat looks.

I suppose it *was* a dumb question. The similar impossibilities mentioned in most alchemical texts are treated by modern commentators as metaphor for a purely psychological transmutation; most magic is, these days, when only allegorical angels dance on the head of New Age pins. Depending on the inclination of the magician, there are a number of different ways to interpret what *La Tesoraria* says, ranging from simple animal sacrifice and bestiality to a rather airy-fairy congress of the spirit, but the book itself is quite explicit. *La Tesoraria* calls for human sacrifice. I wondered which allegorical reading Julian was going to give its injunction when he got there. (In this it is not, as I've said, out of line with other medieval grimoires, whose recipes suggest that no one short of Giles de Rais has ever properly mastered the Black Arts, but it is also not particularly legal, ethical, moral, or PC. Of course, neither is your classic floor-model magician.)

I'd given up on *La Tesoraria* and was just about to have to choose between *Cats Are Angels Too* and *New Aeon Crystal Power* when Ironshadow showed up to save me from the sin of literary criticism.

"And good morning to you," he said cheerfully. He was looking particularly pleased with himself, which meant that *somebody*, at least, was having a good HallowFest.

"I may rise, but I'm damned if I'm going to shine," I answered with moderate good grace, and his grin widened. Ironshadow has enormous white teeth that make him look as if he's capable of eating trees for breakfast. His smile is particularly unsettling if you have the least bit of a guilty conscience, but fortunately mine was almost clear.

"My, my—did we get up on the wrong side of the van this morning?" He set his suitcase down on top of his card table and popped the locks. I watched as he arranged his last few *athamés* and the other samples of his art on the length of black velvet: single-edged, double-edged . . .

But nothing that could have made that hole in Jackson Harm, my helpful brain reminded me.

I decided to think about the late Jackson Harm and how he got that way for a while, as it was more fun than thinking about Lark, Julian, or whether I was still going to be friends with Maidjene after I told her about that gypsy switch I'd pulled with the HallowFest records.

A gypsy switch is where you hand someone a package—usually containing valuables—and they hand it back. Or so you think, but the package you get back is never the one you handed over, and the substitution is called after its originators by those in the bunco know. The image set up a faint nagging warning in my backbrain. A gypsy switch—had someone swapped one knife for another to make the knife that killed Hellfire Harm disappear?

And if so, how? What killed Harm had left a distinctive entry wound, to say the least; the knife that made it would be instantly recognizable. But I was the only one who'd seen it. Nobody else would associate a *kukri* with foul play, so if the killer had helped himself to somebody else's knife to do the deed, its owner might be walking around with it this very moment, having no idea that he was carrying around evidence in a murder investigation.

And tomorrow he—along with everyone else here at Paradise Lake—would go home, and the chain of evidence would be broken forever.

As a theory it was pretty unworkable, since Harm had been killed early Saturday morning and not too many people had been around then to loan the murder weapon to Harm's killer, but I was equally willing to entertain the theory's evil twin: that the killer had stashed the knife he'd used among others somewhere here at the Festival, hiding it in plain sight.

Competing theories—all in need of more baking than they'd currently had—jostled and proliferated in my head until the only thing I was sure of was that I wanted to turn HallowFest inside out looking for something I wasn't even sure I could put a name to. I wondered if our friends the police felt the same way.

"Reality to Bast," Ironshadow said.

"You call this reality?" I snarked. "I could pull a better reality out of a hat."

He just grinned in a self-satisfied way and settled himself behind his table. "You hear they're out there dragging the lake this morning?"

"What?" I hadn't seen anything like that when I came in. I hoped my co-religionists weren't giving Bat Wayne too much grief.

"They were just getting things set up when I went by. Big-old gasoline generator, winch, seining net. Going to pull up every carp and Coke can in the whole damn thing, take forever, and find them exactly zip."

And Maidjene would be right there reminding them about our Fourth Amendment rights, no doubt. I had an appointment with her that I didn't want to keep, and the addition of the Sheriff's Department to the mix didn't sound calculated to improve her forbearance or the idle hour.

"And speaking of guns and their nuts, have you heard anything about Larry?" I asked.

"He wasn't booked. Jeannie had to go down to the station in Tamerlane and pick him up, though." Ironshadow looked disapproving; Maidjene had a lot of friends and none of them liked Larry.

"Is he still here?" I asked. It would have been lovely to be able to pin Hellfire Harm's murder on Larry, but I really found it hard to imagine Larry stabbing anybody, although I could certainly see him *shooting* someone, probably by mistake.

"The Warwagon," Ironshadow remarked to the ceiling, "has not left the grounds, either yesterday or today. It would, of course, be amazing if it had, with four flat tires, but . . ."

"You didn't!" I yelped, laughing in spite of myself.

Ironshadow turned the blandest of bland gazes upon me. "That would be vandalism," he said solemnly, "which would be illegal. And as young Lawrence has not so far disturbed the peace of the Festival, it would be wrong of someone to chastise him."

I hoped Larry Wagner had Triple-A. I hoped they'd send someone who could either patch a flat on a Winnebago or tow one. And while it was wrong of me to take such unholy delight in Larry's probably-deliberately-engineered misfortune, I did feel that the punishment fit the crime.

So what crime had Harm committed to merit *his* punishment—and did it fit as well?

I was abruptly cross again and might have said something regrettable, but fortunately Julian finally showed up. He was dressed, as always, in severe and funereal black—clerical collar, hammertail coat, trousers to match the coat, and glossily shined shoes. He stood in the doorway of the barn's second floor, polishing his glasses with a handkerchief and blinking as his eyes adjusted to the relative gloom after the bright light outside.

Julian is not a creature for bright light. He looked jarringly out of place here, but tomorrow the creature of the night would return to the night.

I reminded myself that I really ought to bear in mind that all this Gothic nonsense about Julian was the product of my imagination and not his lifestyle. People aren't like works of fiction, with every piece matching perfectly. At some point in his life Julian must have gone to kindergarten and the dentist and had birthday parties and the flu just like everyone else. Had what mainstream America would call a *normal* life.

In theory.

He was looking toward my table, and so he was looking toward the windows. The light shone full on his face; smooth skin, smooth shaven (it seemed unreasonable to think that Julian shaved, but he must) that granted the superficial illusion of youth, but the tiny lines around his eyes revised his age upward from Generation X to Woodstock I. It was odd to think of Julian not only subject to time but as a person somewhere near my age, although I'd known he wasn't young. If nothing else, it takes time to master the magical skills that I knew he had. He put his glasses back on and came toward me.

"I'll watch the table for a while," Julian said. "There isn't anything else to do here," he added, dismissing the Festival and all its workshops with a shrug.

"Sure," I said. I started to tell him about the morning's transactions and the state of the stock, but Julian wasn't interested. He came around the table, sat down in the chair I'd been standing beside, and pulled *La Tesoraria* over to him, much as if I wasn't there. I could smell cinnamon and oranges; the formula from *La Tesoraria*.

If I hadn't still been morbidly sensitive I might have stayed, since, interesting or not, I'd missed the start of the workshops and didn't want to come in late. But this particular morning that feat of detachment was beyond my skill.

When I got to the first floor of the barn it was practically empty. Both doors of the barn were open to the October sunshine and a perfunctory hand-lettered sign announced that the workshop on "Finding Your Faerie Guardians" had been moved to the Bardic Circle. Further investigation revealed that the Woods Walk had met down by the bridge and would be gone for two hours, and "Ritual Swordsmanship" had been moved from the Lake Meadow to the lower parking area. There was a notation "due to Faschist [sic] Pigs" on the paper after that one. From the direction of the lake I could hear a lawnmower-on-steroids sound that was probably the winch engine, and a lot of businesslike male voices making shouted conversation over the din.

I looked around. Nobody in sight through either door or the windows. I turned around and went through the door to one of the main bunkrooms.

There are two of them, and they occupy most of the first floor of the barn. Each one sleeps around thirty, in two rows of double-decker bunks. I remembered Maidjene saying that one of the rooms had been given over to parents with small children (Iduna sprang to mind). Out of a lunatic sense of expedience she'd made it the one nearer the bathrooms; I went into the other one.

It showed the signs of untidy overoccupancy by a tribe not noted, by and large, for its housekeeping or wilderness survival skills. Sleeping bags were in the minority; most of the bunks were piled with patchwork quilts and satin-edged blankets, Holofil comforters with Kliban print designs, and assorted stuffed animals. The luggage consisted of duffel bags and backpacks and plain cardboard boxes and the odd Samsonite suitcase; ritual robes were hung off the foot of most of the upper bunks, uneven hems trailing on the floor.

It was a familiar homely clutter; one I was so used to that in any year but this I would have walked in and simply taken it for granted. This was the way things were.

But this year was different in so many ways. I found

myself thinking that there was no way I could search this mess even if I wanted to. It looked like an explosion in the Department of Lost Luggage.

All but one corner.

There were—I blinked, but they didn't go away—*footlockers* at the foot of two bunks in the corner and the beds were made up with black satin sheets. There was a banner hung on the wall between the two footlockered bunks, and another one covered the window. Everything was militarily neat and precise.

I moved closer, carefully negotiating the encroaching-or-escaping collections of personal possessions. Someone had brought what looked like six cases of Classic Coke with them this weekend and was doing pretty well at emptying them, if the clear trash bag full of empties was any guide. Considering that I was surviving the weekend more or less entirely on smoked oysters and warm Diet Pepsi I wasn't in any position to throw stones, but still, there are limits.

I had no idea what I was looking for or why, and I even more certainly had no right to look for it—only a nagging unsatisfied might-be hubris that told me I had to search for . . . something.

I suspected I'd found the Klingon Wiccans.

The Klingons had made their encampment into a complete home away from home. There was a rug on the floor—gray, shaggy, and real fur—and a small table in the corner with a candle in a glass chimney on it. I looked up and realized the banner on the wall wasn't quite what it seemed. The stylized bird design was composed of knife sheaths, and every one of them was filled.

I reached up toward it.

"What do you think you're *doing?*"

It was the Klingon woman with the hubcaps, the one I'd seen on Saturday with the elaborate leather armor almost as impressive as Orm Klash's. She'd either slept in her latex appliances or found some way to put them on even under HallowFest's rudimentary sanitary conditions, and I don't think she'd internalized the love-feast protocols of the New Aquarian Frontier.

"Hi, I'm—"

"You stupid touchy-feely fuck—you were going through our stuff!" She hadn't waited for an answer; Lady Macbeth had her own script and she was happy with it, thank you very much. She took another step toward me and I could smell the sharp chemical tang of cheap-cured leather mixed with the need for a shower and some sweet resiny scent I couldn't immediately identify.

"Look," I began, gesturing toward the banner, planning some only slightly mendacious explanation.

She backhanded my hand away from it. I am not a small woman, but the Klingon lass had a few inches and a lot of pounds on me and she was wearing armor to boot. The metal studs on her wrist-guard dug into my skin with a bright, stinging pain and I heard her grunt: with satisfaction, with exertion.

I have received worse slaps from worse people, and because of that, I no longer handle being threatened in a particularly sensible manner. The spider kiss of adrenaline sang through my veins. I lunged for the banner again and this time ripped it off the wall, too furious to be wise.

I whipped the banner toward me like a matador playing the bull and its sheaths spilled knives. Blades hit the floor while others, still caught in their sheaths, clanged against the bed frame as the felt wrapped around it. "Sorry," I said, in a tone that turned the word into a threat. She'd struck where I was brittle, and I'd shattered.

Lady Macbeth was probably more terrorized by that than my grabbing her national flag. I think she tried to run for it but there wasn't a lot of room between the bunks; what she did instead was shove me hard enough to knock me off balance. I barely managed to turn the fall into a hasty collapse to the mattress. It gave us both a breathing space; I was still angry, but now not crazily so.

The Klingon hesitated over the spilled knives.

"Step away from the little lady," a high voice quavered uncertainly.

Lady Macbeth and I both froze.

Larry Wagner was standing in the center aisle near the door. He was still dressed in the Weight Watchers version of paramilitary chic, but, unlike the last time I'd seen him, he was holding a gun. I wondered if Ironshadow would hear me if I screamed.

"Jesus!" said the Klingon.

I endorsed the sentiment if not the deity. It takes an enormous amount of either chutzpah or stupidity to go around brandishing a gun just after the local Sheriff's Department has spent the night asking you with all due politeness if you've shot somebody.

"Oh, put that away, Larry," I snapped in irritated relief. I was betting on stupidity. "Move!" I barked at the Klingon, who took the opportunity to bolt out from between the bunks. She looked like she'd be happy to get the hell out of here completely if Larry weren't standing in her way.

I didn't have that kind of problem. I walked over to Larry and belatedly realized that someone who'd walk up to a man who was holding a gun intending to clock him one was not as grounded on the Earth Plane as she might think.

But I do not take well to being threatened.

"Good thing I had this, huh?" Larry said. "Right?"

I barely did not hit him. "Put it away." The gun was tiny and brightly chromed; it was hard to take something that looked like it came out of a box of Cracker Jack seriously. Or maybe it was just Larry I was having trouble taking seriously.

Larry put his combat-booted foot up on one of the mattresses and pulled up his pant leg, exposing hairy calves and a concealed holster that had that "loving hands at home" look. He actually patted the gun as he tucked it away.

My hands were starting to shake from the aftermath of the adrenaline rush, and I was beginning on a headache for the same reason. It's amazing what your body can do to you if you give it half a chance.

"Good thing I came along, right?" Larry said. "I saw you heading this way and if I hadn't followed you, you'd be in real trouble now."

There was something childishly gleeful about the iteration, and I realized that if I didn't get Larry out of here reasonably quickly Lady Macbeth would realize he wasn't all that dangerous and either come and clock him herself or go for reinforcements. You might respect the damage he could do, but you'd never respect Larry. I glanced back. She was standing with her back pressed against the wall, her expression a mix of vulnerability and growing anger.

"Come *on*, Larry," I said. "Walkies."

I grabbed him by a fold of his jacket and towed him out of the bunkroom. He followed me willingly, as if we were allies in some grand adventure, and I decided that the barn's main room wasn't far enough away. For one thing, there was a couch out there, and Larry is far from trustworthy around couches, especially when he feels you owe him something.

We went outside.

The sound of the winch down by the lake increased exponentially as soon as we were in the open air. Straight ahead was the wide dirt path with the cabins on the left and bushes on the right. The lake was beyond the cabins; ahead, the road went on past the cabins and then split, half doubling back behind the bushes, heading down until it reached the parking lot, half going straight on past Helen Cooper's house. It looked like a reasonably safe and public place to have a conversation with Larry Wagner. I didn't like Larry, but I prefer being in the right at all times and noblesse oblige until proven guilty was part of that.

I looked back. Lady Macbeth hadn't followed us. I turned around, waiting for Larry to say something and reining in my temper. Larry regarded me with the sort of limpid brown eyes that make people want to take up vivisection of small helpless animals. There was a kind of desperation in the way he waited, as if he expected me to guess why he'd come after me. I could not understand why Maidjene had ever married him, but we so rarely understand what it is that people see when they look at other people.

The sun was warm enough that I contemplated taking off my parka, and remembered that I'd been in these clothes, what with one thing and another, since Saturday morning. I ought to get my stuff out of the cabin while I knew where Julian was and maybe take a bath in the sink.

It finally became obvious that Larry wasn't going to say anything.

"Did you want something from me?" I said, as politely as I could manage under the circumstances.

"You've got to talk to her for me. She'll listen to you. Hell, she's always listened to you; anyone but her husband."

"What do you want me to say?" I asked. I kept my face bland and my voice neutral. The discipline of eyes and face is the earliest survival mechanism, gained by instinct under siege.

"*You* think of what to say!" Larry said vehemently.

"You and all your smart-mouth friends making her think I wasn't good enough for her—*you* figure out what to say to change her mind."

I stared at Larry blankly. I had accepted the fact of Maidjene and Larry's divorce so thoroughly that it took me a moment to realize that Larry hadn't.

"You tell her I still love her just like I always did—Wagner & Wagner, just like it started out; I don't want her going off like that." Larry stopped abruptly, breathing hard. His face, pale and pasty from junk-food diets and indoor weekends, was turning red; his breathing had quickened.

What could I say that was both kind and honest? Never kick a man when he's down, as the saying goes; he might have a gun.

"I think that Maidjene has probably pretty well made up her mind about things," I said.

"She doesn't mean it!" Larry said desperately. "She needs me—nobody else is going to take her in—she's just in one of her moods. She'll listen to you."

Not if I told her to go back to Larry she wouldn't, I bet. I wished I wasn't here listening to Larry whipsaw between insult and pleading; a man who despised what he needed.

"Larry, I can tell her to be sure she's thought things out thoroughly, but . . ."

"I don't *want* you to tell her to think! I want you to tell her she's making a big mistake. She thinks— She thinks I don't love her—but I do. I always have." His face twisted up in earnest and got redder. For a moment I thought he was going to cry, and I tried to feel sympathy for him and failed. Maybe Maidjene had finally failed at that as well.

"Larry, you've been making passes at everything in sight for as long as I've known you, and right in front of her—is that love?"

"Men aren't like women," Larry said. "I didn't do anything anybody didn't want me to. Philly understood that—

at least she did until she started up with all this Goddess crap. It was bad enough when she was Born Again—and now I'm supposed to believe that a bunch of girls standing around naked in my bedroom can make something happen just by wishing and Philly tells me that some *god* told her to get a divorce?"

I'd bet dollars to broomsticks that Maidjene had said no such thing.

"Larry, I'm sure the two of you were very happy once. But people change, and Maidjene—"

"Don't you go calling her that! Her name's Phyllis. Phyllis Eileen Wagner, just like on our marriage license, and she's *my wife.*"

He said it the way he might say: *my car,* with as much entitlement and as little honest affection. And I was tired of this pointless conversation anyway.

"Look, Larry, what exactly is it that you want me to do? She doesn't want to be married to you and I can understand that: *I* wouldn't want to be married to you. Hell, I don't know why she married you in the first place—"

"Oh, you just think you're the cutest little thing, don't you?" Larry snarled. The down-home twang in his voice was stronger by the minute: he sounded now the way he looked, like a nasty-minded good ol' boy, the kind of reactionary that doesn't want to be bothered with the facts.

"If this is the way you ask for favors, Larry, I'd just love to see you try to piss somebody off," I snapped. "I couldn't do what you want even if I wanted to. Now leave me alone."

I already felt guilty; sufferance is not among my virtues. I tried to tell myself that a tonic dose of disenchantment would be the best thing for Maidjene's soon-to-be-ex but I couldn't really make myself buy it. What I needed was someplace to go that would put a final end to the conversation. I settled for walking off down the road. Maybe Helen Cooper would give me another cup of coffee.

"Who are you to judge me?" Larry yelled after me. "Who do you think you are?"

I stopped and turned around. You cannot reason with people like Larry, but sometimes, out of a despairing sense of civic duty, I still try.

"I'm me," I said. "Everybody judges. It's called being alive."

"Yeah, well, you didn't like it so much when Hellfire Harm did it, did you? Called you Satanists and said you'd all better come to Jesus? You stuck-up bitch—maybe you didn't kill him but I bet you're glad he's dead. You're too gutless to pop him yourself but you'd sure love for *some-body* to do it; fall all over yourself crowning them hero of the fucking Revolution and be *happy* to do what they wanted . . ."

They could probably hear him on the other side of the lake. I saw the Klingon woman watching us nervously from the doorway, and when I looked up I saw Ironshadow looking down from the second-floor window. At least there were plenty of witnesses.

"Larry, go away," I said. At least I could eliminate one suspect: if Larry were the killer there was no way he'd back off from calling in the "favor" now.

He smiled nastily. "Fine. I'll go away and leave you alone, Miss Witch Queen of the Goddamn Universe. But you aren't going to like what happens when I tell Philly about what you've done. You aren't going to be so high and mighty then."

We are none of us without guilt. The first thing I thought was that Larry had found out about my switching the Festival's registrations, and I almost fell into the trap of trying to reason with him that disclosure would serve no purpose. But he might be bluffing. Or he might be thinking of something else entirely. And at any rate, it was blackmail.

"Fuck off, Larry," I said, and turned again in the direction of Mrs. Cooper's house.

Larry trotted after me at a safe distance, trying to restart the conversation—which, since it had consisted of whining threats from Larry and abortive reasonableness from me, wasn't something I could see any point to, even if Larry hadn't succeeded in pissing me off royally. I would have preferred to feel compassion and understanding, but what I felt mostly was embarrassment. I wished he'd go away.

When I finally reached Mrs. Cooper's house, Larry was still following, but now it didn't matter. Lark's dark red Harley was parked beside the porch, and Lark was straddling it, talking to Mrs. Cooper. I walked faster.

Lark grinned when he saw me. The grin widened when he looked past me; I glanced back over my shoulder and saw Larry shuffling off toward the parking lot, trying to look as if that had been his destination all along.

"I sure hope he wasn't planning on going anywhere—not with four flat tires," Lark said when I reached him.

"And good morning to you, too," I said. I wondered who'd done the actual slashing of the Winnebago's tires, though at the moment I was almost willing to have done it myself.

"Well, I can't spend all day here chattering," Mrs. Cooper said to Lark. "You just go and do what I told you and you'll be fine." She went in the house and closed the door.

The deep porch cast the front of the house into shadow, making it possible to see inside. Through the lace curtains at the window I could see Mrs. Cooper cross the dining room toward the kitchen.

"Look," Lark said to me. "You want to go out for lunch or something? There's a diner up the road."

I checked my watch. Noon. If Deputy Pascoe had got

off work at six o'clock this morning, she probably wouldn't be hanging around the diner now. Not that I had a guilty conscience or anything.

"Sure," I said.

"Hop on," Lark said. I guessed we'd forgiven each other for last night.

I swung my leg over the seat behind him. He handed me a crash helmet, a bowl-shaped thing painted the same deep heart's blood color as the farings on his bike. I Velcroed the chinstrap up and put my arms around his waist. Lark kicked the bike to life and swung it around, heading down the dirt road in the direction of County 6 again.

There's something about riding a bike that's like flying. Your mind turns the engine roar into silence and you seem to glide effortlessly through the world. Everything's close enough to touch, and it's as if the bike goes away too, and all that's left is you and the speed and the wind.

I rested my cheek against Lark's denimed shoulder and tried not to obsess on what Larry might tell Maidjene and who was going to yell at me when I got back to Paradise Lake and how Arioch's blood had looked in the moonlight. I wondered if I'd come back here next year. I wondered if I'd be let to come back next year. I wondered if there'd *be* a next year. If the Klingon woman complained to Maidjene and was willing to complain to the Gotham County Sheriff's Department, they'd probably arrest Larry for waving a gun around today, but while I was even willing to believe that he'd given or sold or loaned the gun that had done last night's shooting, there was no way he could have either done the shooting himself or stabbed the Reverend Jackson Hellfire Harm Friday night. Not without bragging about it today.

The motorcycle's engine vibrated up through my spine, making my scalp tingle. I wished, now, that I'd gotten a better look at the Klingon knife banner I'd had my hands on so briefly. My impressions weren't very clear, but it seemed to me that it'd been heavier than it would have been if it contained ordinary flat-bladed knives. Had one of the *objets decoratifs* been a *kukri?* And had Orm Klash loaned it out—or had it borrowed?

But no. The Klingons had gotten to HallowFest *after* Jackson Harm's body was found and long after he'd been stabbed; none of them could be the murderer. But what if they'd found, or been given, or had the knife substituted for one of their own *later?*

We arrived.

9

We settled into a front booth in the diner where Lark could keep an eye on his bike. The waitress came. I ordered coffee. Lark ordered beer.

"So was Larry giving you a hard time or what?" Lark said.

"He wanted me to talk Maidjene into going back to him," I said. I wondered what Lark and Mrs. Cooper had found to talk about.

"Asshole," Lark said comprehensively.

The beer and coffee arrived and we ordered—bacon cheeseburger platters all 'round. I told my arteries I'd be virtuous later, although living in the Big Apple is such a health hazard by itself that it hardly matters what else you do with your life.

"So," I said, when the waitress had gone. "Where are you heading off to tomorrow?"

"Down to the city." "The city" means New York, always; every other local habitation has a name, but New York is the only city.

Lark pulled the sugar caddy over to him and began grouping the little packets by the designs on the back. "I figured it was time to start over. You know—live down my mistakes and all that?" he said with a crooked grin.

"Sure," I said, though I couldn't think of any mistakes Lark had made lately. As far as I knew, the biggest mistake in his life was his parents', who had named him Elwyn. I stared at the acreage for sale across the road. There was a stand of white birch, all in yellow fall leaves.

Nothing gold can stay. Robert Frost. Márgarét, are you grieving/Over Goldengrove unleaving? Gerard Manley Hopkins. I felt as if I was saying good-bye, and I didn't know why.

"You know," said Lark, "I was kind of hoping I could work with you, you know? I had a group out in Anaheim, but after what happened they decided not to know me. Big talk. *All* talk," he added a little bitterly. "Some justice."

After *what* had happened? Whatever it was, clearly it was something he thought I already knew.

"It's better than no justice, I suppose," the half-remembered tag of an old "I, Claudius" springing to mind. Lark snorted eloquently. He finished his beer and called for another and I started to worry about riding back with him. We were probably about five miles from the campground; walkable, if long. I could make up my mind later. Lark drank half the second beer in one pull, straight from the bottle.

"God, I missed that. Look, who are you—"

The burgers arrived.

Who are you working with? he'd been going to say. Who was my working partner? A reasonable question, since everyone but a Ceremonial Magician had one. Would it be him? It was a question I'd been asking myself all weekend; a question I'd had in the back of my mind ever since I'd accepted the reality of the split from Changing. But now that he'd brought up a subject I was determined to talk to him about anyway, I found myself unable to continue with it, tongue-tied as a nervous virgin. Which we were not, to each other, in any sense.

So why couldn't I get off the dime?

Lark devoted himself to lunch in a fashion that suggested he hadn't been fed for weeks, but he had to come up for air sometime.

"So who are you going to be working with?" he said when he did. "Anybody I know?—not that I know anybody out here anymore."

"Why did you leave?" I said. It wasn't a question I'd thought I had any interest in the answer to, but I've been wrong before.

"I was young and stupid." His inflection gave the sentence neither regret nor irony.

"And you're older and wiser now?"

"Older, anyway. And Second. And Long Island," Lark said, reminding me that he was not only a ranking member of our tradition, but that he came from the same branch: the Gardnerians who could trace their lineage back to the Long Island Coven founded back in the sixties by Rosemary and Raymond Buckland, whose spiritual mandate—for what that was worth—had come from Gerald Gardner himself.

"You know we work well together," he added.

"Not for ten years. It'd be like starting over."

"You'd be starting fresh with whoever you pick."

"I haven't even made up my mind. I've never run a coven."

"I have. Goddammit, Bast, you've been around for years and watched everything Belle does—what are you waiting for, a handbook?"

"Yeah, well, maybe," I admitted.

"So write one. What about it?" Lark said.

He was doing nothing more than echoing my own thoughts back to me, but things seemed to be moving too fast; everything he said sounded as if it ought to be the right answers, but I felt as if I were being pushed into making a choice that I wouldn't make if I had time to think about it.

"Lark, you've just gotten back. It's been a long time; this isn't the time to be making decisions like that. I mean, somebody stabbed Jackson Harm, and—"

"And you think I did it," Lark said, deadly flat. I felt a warning prickle of the little hairs on the back of my neck. "Hell, why not—what's a little murder among friends?"

He thought I already knew. I didn't, but I managed to piece it together from what he said then. He'd been working in a family-planning clinic in Orange County, California, which had gotten the same flack that clinics everywhere get in these antichoice times. And then one day it had burned in a highly suspicious fashion.

"So I figured if Heather Dearest could bomb a GYN clinic she ought to expect a little Christian charity in return."

And Lark had felt that biblical retribution was in order. An eye for an eye. A building for a building.

"Local merchants wouldn't let the place reopen—bad for business, they said, and everybody knowing that good old Reverend Heather Grace Barrows had been yapping about 'cleansing fire from heaven' in her sermons for weeks, so 'who will rid me of this turbulent priest,' right?" Lark snarled. And two years ago this month—they make you stick close during your probation—he'd been released from the Orange County Correctional Facility after serving eighteen months of a three-year sentence for arson.

"Honest to Goddess, Lark," I said helplessly. It was, I supposed, justice of a sort—bomb a clinic, get bombed in return—providing any of what I'd heard was true. But it was vigilante justice, and a society which allows individuals to take the law into their own hands is doomed.

"The bimb wasn't home. Nobody was; I checked—which was more than she did for us. And that tax-dodging bitch could afford a new coat of paint."

"But Lark—"

"And you know what the real joke was?" He looked into

my eyes, smiling his twisted grin. "Everybody in Ocean Circle'd been saying it was time for some Instant Karma — only when it came down, all of a sudden it was nobody's idea but mine."

Oh, Lark, what did you expect? I shook my head sadly. Even if what he'd done had been legal as church on Sunday he probably wouldn't have gotten the support he'd been expecting—as I knew to my cost. Our Community isn't a Community, not really. It's an assemblage of chance-met fellow travelers, singularly unwilling to make moral judgments.

"Judge not, lest ye be judged," the rabbi from Galilee is rumored to have said, and his followers have always assumed it was a command, even as they ignored it. But it's not a command. It's a reality. Judge and be judged. No one here gets out alive.

"So you just stay wrapped up in your sanctimonious little shroud with that silver-plated virgin looking down on you from Heaven, sweetheart. Some of us are living in the real world."

Lark dug a twenty out of his pocket and tossed it on the table. He was out of the booth and halfway to the door before I realized what was happening.

"Come back here you son of a *bitch!*"

I caught up with him just as he reached his bike.

"Don't you talk to me about the real world!" I said, grabbing his arm. "And don't you go using it as an excuse."

I didn't have the slightest idea what I meant. All I knew was that all the adrenaline left over from the Larry and the Klingon had finally found a home.

"Maybe I did do it," Lark taunted. "Yeah, here I am: the Horned Avenger, doing what you're too scared to!"

I wished I knew why everybody was so convinced I wanted Harm dead. Before this weekend I'd barely known he existed.

"I just love the odor of sanctity you're exuding—is that a new cologne?" We're never so eloquent as when we're flaying old lovers. "What makes you think that murder has suddenly become a moral act?"

"It's better than moral cowardice," Lark said. "You're afraid to stick up for what you believe in—and you're afraid of anyone who does."

"I sure as hell hope that pedestal is comfortable," I snarled back. "Seeing as you're going to spend so much time up there."

Lark jerked away from me and swung his leg over the seat of the bike.

"*Did* you kill him?" I said to Lark's back, more to piss him off than because I cared about the answer just now.

"Sure," Lark said. He kicked the bike to life. "I shot him right through the heart."

I watched Lark skim off down the road. It wasn't me he was angry with, although the realization wasn't particularly comforting. I was standing in for Ocean Circle, and everything they hadn't done.

I hadn't known about Lark's prison record until just now, but once I did, it didn't take much of a leap of imagination to wonder if someone who'd firebombed one anti-abortionist might not have killed another. It would have been damned unlikely that Harm *wasn't* anti-Choice, given the rest of his platform. Or Harm could have recognized Lark—I imagine Lark's trial and conviction had been front-page news with pictures in the *Godbotherer's Gazette.*

But Lark—who'd been mad enough not to choose his words carefully—had said that Harm had been shot, just as Larry had. It was a reasonable assumption, but it wasn't the truth. Harm had been stabbed.

Was it an ignorant-therefore-innocent assumption? Or had Lark learned tactics in the last ten years?

I went back inside the diner.

* * *

Everyone stared at me when I went in. I went back to the booth, sat down, and tried to ignore them. The dishes hadn't been cleared away yet. I tried my coffee. It was cold.

"Have a fight with your boyfriend?" the waitress said sympathetically. "I could ask Charlie can he give you a lift as far as Tamerlane. You could get a bus from there."

"Thanks," I said, "but I don't think I'm going that far." I looked at the ruins of two Double Bacon Cheeseburger Deluxes and decided I could call the campground to see if Ironshadow or someone could come and get me. Or maybe there was something approaching a taxi service. Or I could walk it, which would at least have the advantage of keeping me out of trouble. "Do you think I could have some more coffee and the dessert menu?"

Lark came back about the time I was finishing my apple pie à la mode and a third cup of coffee.

"You coming back to the campground or not?" he said ungraciously.

"You want dessert?" I said without looking up. Lark waited until it was obvious even to him that I wasn't moving and slid back into the opposite side of the booth.

I had the hopeless feeling that today's lunchtime theater was going to be a report on somebody's desk before dinner. I wondered what they'd say and do. The fact that I wasn't going to be the one in trouble was scant comfort. I finished my pie, although it wasn't easy.

"I'm not going to apologize," Lark said.

"So don't," I said.

Lark stopped the bike by Mrs. Cooper's house and I got off. He fishtailed around in a spray of dirt and gravel and sped off again. I thought he'd come back eventually, but I wasn't completely sure.

I wanted to go home. I wanted my own shower and my

own bed and my own refrigerator full of beer. I wanted to stop dealing with murder and other quaint native folkways not my own. The more I considered Jackson Harm's unsought quietus, the more I thought the identity of his killer wouldn't be anything I'd end up wanting to know.

I should go talk to Belle and arrange for Lark's crash space out of a vindictive sense of moral superiority. I should go up and take over the table from Julian. I should go find Maidjene and give her a pound of flesh.

What I did do was go back to the bungalow.

You could lock the door from the inside, so I did. I wanted a bath and compromised with an unsatisfactory scrub in the rusty sink and a change of clothes, which made me feel a little better but not much. I'd never really gotten unpacked, so it didn't take long at all to bundle my stuff back into the duffel I'd brought it in.

Maybe I could talk Julian into packing and leaving tonight. He already had his Ironshadow blade; picking it up had to be the reason he'd come to the Festival. The selling was all but over and we could load the van tonight and be back in the city by four A.M. at the latest. Julian hadn't wanted to be here in the first place, and by now neither did I.

Having a plan cheered me up; I took my duffel down to the van and loaded it in, feeling optimistic enough to roll my sleeping bag up and tie it, ready to go. But by the time I got back up the hill to the barn, I'd changed my mind again. I didn't want to be here, but I had the superstitious feeling that leaving would be worse—although tomorrow at noon it would become a moot point. Tomorrow at noon the Festival would be over, and everyone would leave.

Including Harm's killer, if he—or she—were one of us. I kept a wary eye out for Larry and any stray Klingons as I headed for the barn.

The news reached me before I reached it.

"Larry Wagner's been arrested!" Lorne said. Lorne was a member of Summerisle—if Maidjene's soon-to-be-ex had been arrested, he'd know.

I stopped and stared at him, and as I stood there wondering what to do, I heard the back door bang and Glitter came running toward me.

"Is it true?" she demanded.

"What?" I stared at her. Maidjene and Belle had followed her out. I walked over toward them. Glitter and Lorne followed.

"It isn't true," she told them.

"They took him away!" Lorne said. Maidjene had been crying, and she started to cry again.

"Why didn't you *tell* me, Bast?" she said.

"I was going to, but . . ." I said.

Maidjene shook her head, shutting me out. "I could have done something!" she sobbed, which even in the confusion clued me that she could not be talking about my stealing the festival records.

"You know what Larry's like," Belle said to Maidjene, soothingly. I looked at Glitter. The expression on her face said that things were not good.

Larry arrested? "What's going on?" I said.

"Larry said this Klingon beat you up," Glitter said. She inspected me critically. "You don't look beat-up."

"A Klingon did not beat me up." I stared at Maidjene. "And you *believed* him?"

Maidjene shook her head. "But she said he had a gun, and she went and told one of the deputies down by the lake, and we couldn't find you, and—"

"It was kind of a mess," Belle admitted. "Everyone was looking for you because you were the only one who'd seen him with the gun besides Rhonda."

Rhonda must be the Klingon.

"I went down to the diner," I said feebly.

"What nobody could figure out was how he still had a

gun," Glitter said with interest. "They found it on him," she amplified.

And possession being nine points of the law, Larry was now getting an even closer look at the judicial system of Gotham County. " 'Still'?" I asked.

"Well, he didn't exactly have permits for the others, so they sort of confiscated all of them," Glitter, mistress of modifiers, said.

"You should have said something!" Maidjene said, and while it was true, I could also not see how it could have changed the course of events, unless I'd talked Rhonda out of reporting Larry.

"I'm sorry," I said.

"Look," said Lorne to Maidjene, "why don't you come on and lie down, okay? They aren't even going to set bail until tomorrow morning, and the sonovabitch sure had it coming. And you've got to go make a statement," he added to me.

I opened and closed my mouth a couple of times, and gave up. Lorne led Maidjene away.

"There somebody still here?" I asked, and Glitter made a rude noise.

"Follow me," she said.

Glitter and I got to ride down to beautiful downtown Tamerlane in the back of one of their green-and-whites so the Gotham County Sheriff's Department could take my notarized statement in comfort. They were not really pleased with the idea that I'd just figured that the firearms display was just another case of Larry being Larry and therefore hadn't bothered to mention it to anybody. My vagueness earned me a long session in a private room with a detective and a stenographer. The room smelled of dust and Lysol and ancient cigarette smoke. The bulb in the ceiling was protected by a wire cage. There was a bat-tered gray table in the middle of the room and four chairs that looked like they didn't want to have anything to do with it. The floor was covered with multiple coats of battleship gray enamel, and the walls were painted a shade of greenish yellow that looked as if it wanted to be chartreuse but didn't have the energy. There was a frosted glass window in the wall opposite the door, and the walls had dingy two-color-process posters explaining the Heimlich maneuver and giving information on the "Cop Shot" hotline. It was just like the last copshop I'd been in, even though that one had been in Manhattan.

I did my best to give them what they wanted, but it was hard to explain to anyone who hadn't been around for the last fifteen years about how Larry had always had guns—usually cheap small-caliber hideouts—and was always showing them off with the zeal of a Fuller Brush salesman. I finally explained that Larry had been trying to get me to effect a reconciliation with his wife, and I'd been so interested in getting out of there that I wasn't thinking very clearly.

Which brought my story around to Lark. Lark with his prison record, Lark with his *motive*—for Jackson Harm's death, if no one else's. My conviction that he was innocent wouldn't carry as much weight as his prison record would.

I told them I left the grounds with a friend. I had to give his name. But I was also able to cite Helen Cooper as a witness that he'd been nowhere near the barn, nor the trouble with Larry.

Finally I got to leave.

When Glitter and I got back to Paradise Lake it was late and so was I. When I got upstairs in the barn there were customers three deep around the Snake's table.

Lark was there, too. I felt a moment of appalled self-consciousness, as if the only thing he and Julian could possibly be discussing was me. It turned out I was right.

I slid in behind the table, next to Julian, who removed his attention from Lark and started making change.

"Where've you *been?*" Lark demanded, at the same time someone else wanted to know if Three Kings Incense was the same as pure frankincense (it isn't).

"Down in Tamerlane, making a statement to the police."

Lark and Julian both stared at me. Lark's mouth had a set expression that reminded me—forcibly—of our lunchtime conversation. I wondered about the chat he and Julian had been having before I got there. It was hard to think of two people who had less common ground. Dionysus and Apollo; Sun and Moon; Wiccan and apostate . . .

"It wasn't what you think," I said feebly. Julian handed me a stack of books to bag. "Larry's been arrested. I had to make a statement."

"About *what?*" Lark asked with suspicious disbelief.

"He had a gun," I said. ("No shit?" one of the customers asked with interest.) "I saw him with it," I added. Which wasn't quite the whole story, but the whole story wasn't for an audience.

"Okay." Now that this had been settled, Lark remembered he was mad at me again. He glanced at Julian.

"He wondered where you were," Julian said to me. His tone was neutral, but I could tell he was amused. "He thought I might tell him." He regarded Lark over the top of his glasses. Lark glared at him, not quite sure of the subtext but knowing he didn't like it.

"I'm right here," I said ungraciously. Then I had to tell somebody why there were three Waite decks on the table and explain why they all had different prices. Albano-Waite; U.S. Games; and shot from original art, if you're interested.

"I'll see you," Lark said, while I was in the middle of that. His inflection made it something in the nature of a vow, but I didn't know which of us he was talking to.

"I'm certain of it," Julian murmured sweetly. I felt my face grow hot and hoped it wasn't as noticeable as it felt. Business picked up further. I started making change and supplying bags and tried to stop thinking about Lark or anything else.

The fin de siècle shopping frenzy was intense but brief; a little later I dumped the last packet of Three Kings Incense into the last red-and-black paper bag and made change for the last customer. The second floor was still crowded, but people were standing around in the open space, not clumped near the tables.

I glanced over at Ironshadow—his table was bare of everything except the museum pieces and he gave me the "thumbs-up" sign that indicated business had been good. Hallie's rack of tie-dyed robes was almost empty, and the baked goods table was completely gone.

"So how'd we do?" I said to Julian.

"Well enough," he said. "Look, are you . . ." There was a pause. "Are you coming back to the cabin tonight?"

Coming as it did, while my mind was full of Lark, what might be a perfectly innocent question seemed remarkably fraught. Was this Julian's bid to retain my favors, or his acknowledgment of my might-be relationship with Lark? I opened my mouth to suggest leaving tonight instead, but finally remembered a good concrete real-world reason why I'd been so reluctant after all to leave tonight. Tomorrow morning Wyler Pascoe would be coming for his books, and I'd promised him I'd be here. I might even find time tonight to get that reading list from Belle.

But that left tonight to get through. And asking Julian whether he wanted me to come back to the cabin tonight would be playing into all those old boy-and-girl games we're supposed to have left behind now that we've entered the Aeon of Horus. So I said, "I haven't made up my mind yet," instead.

Julian smiled coolly and stood up. "I don't think I'm going to go to the party," he said. "I've got some reading to do. You could drop by if it gets too noisy for you." He walked away before I could collect enough brain cells to field a reply.

The sharp snap of the locks on Ironshadow's case jarred me out of my woolgathering. I looked around and saw him closing his case and starting to fold up the table.

"Nothing left to sell," he said happily. "And I've got to hit the road early tomorrow."

Ironshadow lives somewhere in New Jersey—or, as its habitués refer to it, *Fucking*jersey—and has a trip home that is longer by several hours than the one I was facing.

"Good luck," I said. "When do we see you again?"

"I'm going to be in the city for Twelfth Night; maybe then."

"Call me," I said, meaning it. He grinned a toothy troll-grin and picked up his table, chair, and case.

"Too bad about Larry," he said, and his tone made the words into an epitaph, "but that boy was definitely asking for it."

Yeah, a traitor part of my mind said, *but what did he do besides want to be a hero?*

People began to wander downstairs from the selling floor. There was still light in the sky outside, but it was that lucent misleading brilliance that comes just before you realize it's dusk, when things seem very clear but relationships are hard to judge. Eventually it was just me and someone I didn't know well who had a table full of herbs and oils. She started clearing her table and packing her stuff away. It was about time for me to do the same.

The Gotham County Sheriff's Department had not objected to my plans to leave the county, providing I was willing to come back if they asked. I was, even if not very, and at the moment the thought of getting back to the big city had an obsessive glamour to it. Only the thought of packing the truck in the dark—and the knowledge that, come hell or high water, I still had to talk to Maidjene and meet Wyler—kept me here.

I tried to distract myself. Monday would be a short selling day, with a long load-up at the end of it, but I had a pretty good idea of what I needed to leave out for Monday's last-minute impulse shoppers, and I might as well pack the rest of the stuff now. When I got back to New York it'd be early enough that maybe I'd call Lace and we'd have a big Chinese dinner and then maybe cruise her favorite bars.

Unless Lark . . .

Damn Lark. And Julian, too, for good measure.

Meanwhile, I could get together the books I'd promised Wyler, that he might or might not be back to buy. And I still had to ask Belle about getting Lark a place to stay, which meant after that I'd have to go and find *him*, and . . .

I started to work.

Every year it's the same thing; Julian sends more stock than any six Festivals could absorb, on the theory that Goddess forbid he should miss a sale. Every year 90 percent of it goes back to the shop untouched. Julian is not daunted by this—and I did have to admit it would make filling Wyler's shopping list easier, since who but Julian would bring Wicca 101 books to a Pagan Festival where everyone who came had bought and read them years ago?

I found Buckland's *Complete Book of Witchcraft* and Dion Fortune's *Psychic Self-Defense* without much trouble, but I wanted to include *What Witches Do* by Stewart Farrar and I was pretty sure I'd seen Julian take a copy of it off the shelf back in New York. The only question was, where was it now?

I packed while I searched, trying to group titles by subject and get all the remaining copies together into the same box, although since I wouldn't be the one unpacking them in New York there wasn't a lot of reason for me to bother. An inventory to check things off against would have made life ever so much easier, but every year the van is packed at the last minute and there's no time to do one.

It was while shifting the half-full boxes that I came on the full one.

It was under and behind everything, shoved into a corner and sealed, and if I hadn't had a suspicious nature I would have thought it belonged to Paradise Lake and not to me. But I knew this corner had been empty when I set up and so it must be mine.

Right?

The first thing I saw when I slit the tape was a bundle of cloth, which annoyed me. This must be the wizard's robes that I'd spent the morning looking for; I'd known we'd brought a couple and if I could have found them I'd have been able to sell them. I lifted them out. Maybe I could find Gerry sometime tonight and tell him they were here.

Under the robes was an odd collection of things—cheap brass incense holders, some of the eight-inch beeswax candles that we retail for thirteen dollars each (wholesale they're somewhere around $4.50). Not stuff that we wouldn't have brought, but stuff that shouldn't have been packed together. And at any rate, stuff I might be able to sell tomorrow.

I lifted the candles out, annoyed and puzzled, and saw beneath them one of the Ziploc bags that the Snake uses to pack jewelry, specula, and other small objects up in. Some moron—I had my candidates—must have packed the candles on top of a bunch of jewelry, and it was pure luck and not planning that there wasn't something heavy on top of the candles, because beeswax candles are brittle rather than soft and will break given the right encouragement.

Then I took a good look at the bag.

Those who don't believe in the power of the abstract threat reject the power the imaginative mind has over the body. What I saw had no ability to hurt me, but I looked into the box and felt a sudden rush of adrenaline that made my hands shake and my ears ring.

Lying in the bottom of the box in one of the Snake's Ziploc bags was a *kukri.*

It was not like the Tibetan ones. Its three-flanged blade was made of brass or bronze, and the hilt was a plain shaft of white bone—antler, I thought—finished with a flat brass pommel. There was a dark line where the hilt met the blade. It *could* be epoxy. But it was so much more likely that it was blood.

I stared at the knife in the bag. I had no doubt that I was looking at what had killed Jackson Harm. And it was here. In the Snake's stock.

I looked around. The herbalist was gone. There was nobody up here on the barn's second floor but me. I picked up the bag. It was sealed; there was crumpled white tissue bunched loosely around the knife. I broke the seal on the bag. Trapped air huffed out, redolent of clove and bergamot; chypre, cinnamon, and civet . . .

Julian's ritual oil.

There were any number of people who could be wearing a mix like that, I told myself. And it was true, but I knew too many facts to take that easy out. Holding the knife carefully through the bag I held it up and angled it to catch the weak bulb-light. Its entire surface glinted, even the hilt, glossy with the oil that had been used to wipe it clean after it had been used; the reason that it and the bag reeked of the mix now. I sealed the bag shut again and knelt there holding it.

People who've never experienced it talk all the time about feeling desolated, when what they mean is the mild disappointment of a missed opportunity. Real desolation is when you've lost everything, including things you hadn't known you had. Like innocence. Like ignorance, because now I had the answer that I hadn't wanted.

I'd suspected everyone else this weekend, but never Julian—Julian, who had been out of character from first to last, in coming to HallowFest at all and then in everything that followed. Julian, who made no secret of the fact that he was doing *La Tesoraria*—if you knew what the indicators were. And I did, but I hadn't looked until now. Either at Julian, or at the end of the operation, at the two acts that must be performed.

Love and Death. But as metaphor, as simile—not literal, not actual, not real. The language of magic is metaphor. The requirements of the *Tesoraria* were supposed to be allegorical; their accommodation a symbolic one. I did not expect a real death to proceed from the *Tesoraria* work any more than the Catholic expects his priest to hand him a chunk of bleeding human meat at the Communion rail.

And so I hadn't looked at the most obvious suspect— because to me he'd been the least possible suspect. Julian. Who was, first and always, a Ceremonial Magician.

And a killer?

No! He's a magician, and magic is real, but there are LIMITS. Nobody commits MURDER in the name of magic, for Goddess's sake, no matter what their beliefs!

Yet the true magician is amoral, and recognizes no law but his own—that's what the books say, isn't it? What was the distance, really, from my perception of the immanence of the Goddess, to the Klingons' embrace of a culture that never was, to Xharina and Arioch in the moonlight, to . . .

To Jackson Harm, dead not for anything he was or had done, but because his death was the last component of a ritual? I looked down at the knife in my hands. The end does not justify the means, nor the means, the end. Human life must be valued so highly that it can never become a component in a marketplace transaction; not for slavery, and not for murder. Someone had killed Harm, that was simple fact. And the oil on the body would match the oil on the knife, on Julian.

On me, Friday night. I swallowed hard.

But I wasn't sure, I told myself. Not sure enough to make the ghastly unbelievable accusation. Julian could have been performing *La Tesoraria* and Harm could have been murdered, and these two events might have only a psychic connection. Or be sheer coincidence, something I'd seen enough of to believe in as devoutly as I did in magic.

I'd said I was willing to pay any price for justice, back when the question was an abstract one and the price was only friendship. But now the bill had been presented, and the price was higher than I could have imagined. And if I was going to pay it, I had to be sure.

I put the bag with the knife in it into the pocket of my parka, where it seemed to burn with malignant intention. Blood shapes the purpose of the blade for once and all; I could barely imagine the shape of the intent in a blade that had been used to kill. I didn't want to hold it any longer than I had to, for fear of the consequences, yet Julian had been willing to sell it.

That made things even worse, but if one thing was true, the other was, too. The *kukri* had been packed up with the rest of the stock and would have been going back to New York tomorrow, to the glass case in the front of the shop, to end someday in the hands of someone ignorant of what it had been, and what it might still do . . .

If it were the murder weapon.

If Julian was the killer.

I had to know.

But when I left the barn, it was not to confront Julian. I went instead to the beginning of things; to the place I'd been drawn to all weekend. To the pine forest where Jackson Harm had died.

It was dark outside now, and cold. Traffic was all the other way, toward the barn, and light, and dinner. I met no one on my way to the Bardic Circle, and up the hill beyond. The winch and the net were gone from the lakeside. Even the deputies seemed to be gone.

I knelt where the body had lain, and reached for the knife. My fingers were cold and clumsy, and the bag in my pocket was slick and unpleasant to touch. Overheated imagination? Or the exercise of directed intuition that is the gift of every magician and Witch? I laid the bag with the knife in it on the pine needles and breathed slowly, letting my imagination and subconscious build a narrative without censorship from my daylight mind. Guided imagery, the New Agers call it, though the whole point is not to be guided. I called the Guardians to stand around me, and protect me from what I was about to see.

It was the blackest part of night, and Harm was here. Where were the leaflets? His plan had been to distribute them at the gathering; he'd left some with Mrs. Cooper, but he couldn't have counted on her to hand them out.

—Give them to me. I'll pass them out for you.

Who was speaking? I didn't know. The words echoed in the mind's ear, unattributable as a line of print.

—I'll pass them out for you.

Harm had felt no fear, only trust in this ally. He'd given—

He'd taken—

I could see the silver flask glinting in the moonlight; the sportsman's friend.

The flask in the moonlight.

—Here, why don't you . . .

I jerked out of trance state, unable to retain the detachment I needed to be there. The white hilt of the *kukri* on the forest floor seemed to glow balefully in the last of the twilight. There was a coppery taste in my mouth: the fight-or-flight reflex of danger.

The sweet musty undertaste in the wine that first night. I'd never slept better—or more soundly. I hadn't heard Julian get up at all. Who sleeps that soundly in a strange place?

"I didn't kill you." Julian's words to me the following morning. I'd been too embarrassed at the time to pay close attention, but had there been the slightest, most scrupulously accurate stress on the last word of the sentence? *"I didn't kill YOU."* Who, then, if not me? Where were the leaflets? That was the real-world proof I had to have. I could not believe that Harm hadn't brought them with him Friday night. They'd been the whole point.

I picked up the *kukri* and put it back in my pocket.

It was after eight o'clock when I got to the bungalow, and I was shivering inside my parka from standing so long in the chill. It had been easy to get to the Bardic Circle, hard to make myself leave it. Harder still to cross the bridge over the lake to reach the path that led to the bungalows. I was filled with a desperate reluctance to take each step, an unwillingness to force the conclusion. Only an act of will kept me moving forward; the trained will that is the root of magical discipline, the training that links the magician and the Witch.

I could see the light on in the bungalow. I knew that Julian was waiting for me; that he knew I was here. And I knew that I would have to move first; the opening gambit in a chess game that could have no winner. How different were Julian and I, if both of us were willing to sacrifice everything for our beliefs? I opened the door.

Julian had been sitting on a folding stool, reading. The light flashed on his glasses as he looked up, dressed as always in clerical black and white, the collar that would have made Harm trust him on sight, there in those midnight woods.

I tried to speak and couldn't. The room seemed to be filled with reflective surfaces, all dazzling me. The knife against the red cloth. The silver-framed mirror. The lit candle.

And beneath the table, a box.

I knelt before it, moving as if Julian weren't there. It wasn't taped shut; I pulled open the flaps and felt weak with relief when all I saw was wadded newspaper — some stock from the Snake that hadn't made it upstairs.

But there was something wrong with the newsprint. I reached for it. Pulled some out. Saw what I didn't want to see beneath, even while I saw that the newsprint and design on the sheet I held were all wrong for any of the New York papers — and why should Julian have packed anything in pages from the *Tamerlane Gazette Advertiser?*

It was the same newsprint I'd seen wrapped around the silver knife, and where would Ironshadow have gotten a *Tamerlane Gazette* when he was home in New Jersey wrapping his custom orders for delivery at the festival? Julian had unwrapped it to look at it, and wrapped it back up in a fresh sheet of newspaper from the box. That was what I had seen without seeing when I was here before. That was why I'd been afraid.

I stared down at stacks of Harm's pamphlet.

Here. Give them to me. I'll pass them out for you.

"You didn't pass out his pamphlets, Julian," I said without moving. "You have to keep your promises."

"I didn't say *where* I'd pass them out," Julian answered.

I stood up. Every muscle ached. Turning to face him was agony. "You killed him," I said.

"Who?" Julian said calmly. Julian, who'd killed to complete *La Tesoraria.* Completed the work and achieved his result. But when you obtain a bill of divorcement from all that is, what do you have left? What did Julian have left?

"Did you kill Jackson Harm?" I said evenly, because nothing must be subjective, nothing left to interpretation.

"Yes." He turned a page in his book.

"*Why?*" I said despairingly.

"You know why," Julian said reprovingly.

Perhaps I should have been afraid, but I knew Julian too well for that. "It's only a *book*," I said.

"If you don't follow a ritual exactly, don't be surprised when it doesn't work," Julian said. "I knew it would come to this when I started *La Tesoraria*. I was willing to pay the price."

"And what about what Harm paid?" I said.

Julian shrugged. "I didn't choose him."

No. Fate or luck or the guiding intelligence of *La Tesoraria* had done that. And it could as easily have been Maidjene, or Lark, or anyone else who'd been here that night. It could have been me.

"And what will you do now?" I asked him.

"The *Tesoraria* work is over. It's served its purpose. I'll write up my notes." And maybe even publish them—safely, because no one would want to see the truth. Just as I hadn't wanted to.

I looked at Julian. He was watching me with uninvolved interest, the cool dispassion of one who has made the decision that ends decision for all time.

"Would you like a drink?" Julian said.

He lifted a silver flask out of his pocket; the one I'd imagined, though I didn't remember ever seeing it before. A few drops of its contents in my glass of wine had made me sleep. A mouthful had made Harm helpless. What would a glassful do? And if I drank it, who had made that choice?

"No," I said.

Julian shrugged. Disappointed, but that was all. Julian had bargained with the spirits for perfect knowledge, and perfect knowledge casteth away fear.

"And what are you going to do?" he asked me.

"I haven't made up my mind yet," I told him.

But I lied. I knew what I was going to do. All I had to find was the courage.

It took me an hour of driving around Tamerlane to find the sheriff's station again, and the closer I got, the less certain I was of what I should do when I got there.

It seemed so much more likely that the whole thing had never happened. I could throw the knife in the lake; it wouldn't cause any trouble there, and the Sheriff's Department wasn't likely to drag the lake twice. I could forget Julian's confession. It was probably his idea of a joke, anyway, just to see how gullible I was. *I* was the one who professed to believe in magic, after all. Julian professed no beliefs.

It would be so easy to let everything go. Keep my mouth shut for twenty-four hours, and the weapon would be gone, the killer vanished. Gotham County could search forever for motive and weapon, and find neither. There had been no motive. And eventually the investigation would be dropped. Unless I told the Sheriff's Department what Julian had told me.

I parked in the lot beneath the sign that said VISITOR PARKING and went inside.

"I need to talk to Sergeant Pascoe—is she here?" I said to the uniformed man behind the desk. He'd been watching me for trouble from the moment I walked in; I suppose I looked like an accident waiting to happen.

"Can I help you?" the sergeant said. I tried to remember the name of the detective investigating the Jackson Harm case, or even of the one I'd talked to this afternoon. It was after seven—would either of them still be here? Why hadn't I just found a phone and called? I could even have remained anonymous, somehow. Maybe.

"Or Detective Anthony Wayne," I said, retrieving the name from memory. "Is *he* here?"

"Your name?" he asked.

I wrenched at a mental clutch. "Karen Hightower. It's about Jackson Harm."

The names got me a seat in the room where I'd spent most of the afternoon. It was even more depressing at night. I wanted to leave, but it was already much too late. I'd given my name; they had my address. The chess pieces were in motion; the game had to be played out.

Detective Wayne came in.

"Good evening," he said. He was carrying two mugs, looking dapper yet rumpled. "Want some coffee?" He set the cups down on the table and juggled with a notepad. "You're . . . Bast, isn't it?"

"Yes." I gave him points for taking the trouble to get not only the name, but the right one.

He handed me a cup. It was black, and had oily beads on its surface. I drank, and tasted the bitterness in my nose and all along the lining of my throat.

"And you said you wanted to talk to me?"

He sat down next to me at the table. I saw a little cloisonné bat-pin from last summer's big movie pinned to his jacket. So the man had a sense of humor.

"I know something," I heard myself say, insanely. The coffee slopped in the cup as I tried to gesture while holding it, and that made me angry. I'd been through this before. This time was no different.

Tony Wayne waited me out.

"I wanted to tell you something. It's probably nothing." I felt myself trying to remember something I'd known too well a lifetime ago, but the words wouldn't settle into any order. *Ego te absolvo,* and all my sins forgiven. Confession is good for the soul. Wash me in blood and my sins will be whiter than snow.

"Someone told me they'd killed Jackson Harm," I said. I sipped the coffee, and to my disappointment, Detective Wayne didn't jump up and down and demand details. I tried to get his interest. "I've got the knife in the van. It's in a bag."

"Can we look in your van?" Detective Wayne asked noncommittally.

"Sure." I pushed the keys across the table. "Here."

He got up and went over to the door. A deputy who must have been standing just outside leaned in, and they spoke. The deputy took the keys and went off.

Detective Wayne came back over to the table.

"Who told you they'd killed Reverend Harm?" he said.

I wanted to say the name. I tried, but it wouldn't come; I felt myself gag on it, victim of the secular sorcery of shock.

"It wasn't because he was him," I said instead. "It could have been anybody." It could have been me, if Julian hadn't had another use for me—and maybe some human vestige of self-preservation, even then. A last cry for help, in the midst of self-destruction. "The point was, it had to be the first person he saw, just like in the old fairy tales, you see? It was because of *La Tesoraria*—he was doing the ritual in *La Tesoraria* and he got to the end. Julian's a magician, you see—" I'd done it; I'd managed to trick myself into saying his name. I felt my throat close with tears, choking me.

"Julian Fletcher?" Wayne said.

I nodded. It was easier, now. The first betrayal is always the hardest. "Julian Fletcher killed Jackson Harm. He told me he did. I found the knife in our stock. I asked him and he told me."

"When was this?" Wayne said.

There was a knock at the door. The deputy came back in, carrying the *kukri* in its Ziploc bag, now rebagged in an evidence bag belonging to the Gotham County Sheriff's Department. I realized that not only the knife but the bag it was in had just become evidence and thought I ought to care about that more.

"Is this the knife?" Wayne said.

I nodded. "I think it has blood on it. The oil on it will match what's on Harm."

And there was beeswax around the body; could they tell that the candles were ours? That Julian had brought them here for just this purpose?

The knife went out again. Tony Wayne leaned close to me.

"Now listen to me, Bast." There was only a slight hesitation before my name and I liked him for that. "This is important, and we really need a straight answer on this. Are you telling us that Julian Fletcher killed Jackson Harm?"

"Yes," I said, feeling defensive anger. "Ask him yourself. He'll tell you, too."

It was long after midnight when they were done with me, and they kept asking me if there was anyone I could stay with tonight, just as if I weren't up here at a campground with two hundred and fifty of my closest friends, most of whom wouldn't want to know me after this. I thought about Lark. Maybe we had something in common at last.

The door opened, and Fayrene came in with a bag of Dunkin' Donuts and a large coffee. She set them down in front of me.

"We brought Mr. Fletcher in," she said. "They're processing him now. I thought you'd like to know."

I pulled the lid off the coffee. Black. Fayrene reached into her pocket and pulled out a handful of sugar and creamers.

"Can I see him?" I asked. The unshed tears were a hard weight at the back of my jaw.

"No," Fayrene said. There was a pause. "You'll see him soon enough."

I wasn't sure what she meant, but it sounded frightening and final. I pulled the lids off four of the creamers and dumped them into the coffee. Fayrene winced, gently.

"You know," she said, seemingly inconsequentially, "my boy thinks the world of you."

I looked up, startled. She smiled. "Oh, we don't keep many secrets. First he does what he doesn't think I'm going to approve of—then he tells me about it afterward. He told me you were going to pick out some books for him to read?"

"Yeah," I said. "I promised. You have to keep your promises." It seemed important to repeat that, but I wasn't sure who I was telling.

Then I thought of something.

"Fayrene," I said, and there was so much urgency in my voice that she whipped around to face me. "You don't need the HallowFest registrations now, do you? You've got Julian. You've got a *confession.* You don't need them, right?"

She stared at me for a long moment, and I could almost see her thinking.

"No. I guess we don't need them now at that."

That was when I finally started to cry.

What is the demarcation line between reality and fantasy? Was Klash, with his insistence upon being a Klingon, deluded, or merely playing out a role? And what about Julian, who followed the *Tesoraria*'s strictures with murderous exactitude? Where does science—or religion— cross the line into madness? Do the borderlands shift every generation, or are they fixed for all time?

The real question was, could any of us stop what we were doing if we wanted to?

No.

Maidjene couldn't—she'd destroyed her marriage and risked jail to follow what she saw Wiccan law to be. I'd alienated my oldest friend for much the same reason.

For his magic, Julian had killed.

It was a difference not of kind, but degree. The same divergence that causes one Christian to picket a Planned Parenthood clinic and another to bomb it. And we say one is permissible, and the other isn't, as we must.

But if it is, *as* it is, only a difference of degree, then where is the line drawn that makes one act right and the other wrong—the line not of law, but of morality? Where is the border between good and evil? How often does each of us cross it every day, and how can we know when we do?

It was dawn by the time they finally let me leave the sheriff's station, and I didn't go back to the campground. I went to the nearest motel. Lark came later. I never asked him how he'd found me.

On Wednesday morning I found out what Fayrene had meant when she'd said I'd see Julian soon enough. I saw him that day, in the courtroom where the Gotham County grand jury brought in a true bill of murder against Julian David Fletcher, and the case was bound over for trial.

In the end, I spent several more days in Gotham County than I had time or money for, and the trial itself was still in the future. Lark stayed with me a while, and then he left. Wyler Pascoe stopped by, too. I asked him for a favor. He promised he'd do it. I can't remember what else I said to him.

It was a cold, gray, empty day when I finally drove back to Paradise Lake to pick up the Snake's stock. Everyone, even Maidjene, was long gone. It was almost November; the campground was closed. I got the keys to the barn from Mrs. Cooper. We didn't have much to say to each other now.

The inside of the barn was as cold as the outside, and

all the electricity was shut off for the winter. Someone had thrown a sheet over the table on the second floor to keep the remaining merchandise clean. I finished packing and sealing the cartons. I even put the books aside for Wyler; The Snake, I figured, owed them to me. Then I carried everything downstairs to the van. There was one more thing I had to do before I was free to go.

In the fire pit in the Upper Meadow Wyler Pascoe and I burned the two copies of the Tesoraria that the Snake had brought to sell. When the leather binding was reduced to ash I filled the fire pit with the wood he'd brought, and when the fire was burning hot and strong I burned the HallowFest registration forms one by one, along with the pamphlets Jackson Harm had left behind.

> *O yearning heart! I did inherit*
> *Thy withering portion with the fame,*
> *The searing glory which hath shone*
> *Amid the Jewels of my throne,*
> *Halo of Hell! and with a pain*
> *Not Hell shall make me fear again—*

> —*Tamerlane*, Edgar Allan Poe